HOW THE SKIN SHEDS

CHAD LUTZKE

How the Skin Sheds
Copyright © 2023 by Chad Lutzke

Published by Death's Head Press,
an imprint of Dead Sky Publishing, LLC
Miami Beach, Florida
www.deadskypublishing.com

First U.S. Edition

Cover Art: Justin T. Coons

Edited by: Christine Morgan and Anna Kubik

Copyedited by: Kristy Baptist

The "Splatter Western" logo designed
by K. Trap Jones

Book Layout: Lori Michelle
www.TheAuthorsAlley.com

ISBN 9781639511136

Dedicated to Joe R. Lansdale—who taught me to write as if I'm my own genre, dipping a toe into whatever I like. To pay no mind to pigeonholes and trends. To mix the horrifying with the humorous. To hold strong to my punk ethics. To shed one literary skin and be comfortable in the next.

CHAPTER 1

GOT TO Diane's about noon. I could tell by the empty stable and the free-swinging gate that something wasn't right.

The bruised clouds overhead seemed to paint the perfect picture of trouble, which I'd been following all morning like some north star that led to no good.

I hitched Bones to the same post I always did. He didn't seem to like the air either and had spent the last hour huffin' over it, not all that eager to get to my sister's ranch. He had a way about things. A sixth sense. I'd like to think it was that same sixth sense what led him to crush Stewart William's head like a grape underfoot, turning that fool thief into blood wine. A good horse knows an asshole when they see one, and Stewart was starving him—hence the name I later gave the poor beast.

Bones whinnied as I walked toward the porch and saw the front door ajar. Some bad shit had definitely gone down—my worst fear being a wagon full of stiff dicks found a lone woman in the middle of nowhere and I wasn't there to stop them.

I pulled my gun and didn't fuck around, kicked the door wide. Diane faceup was the first thing I saw. Half on the bed, half off, like she was maybe sliding down when rigor mortis set in. The top of her dress had been ripped open, and her breasts spilled out. Where her nipples used to be, there were dark-red circles. Jagged circles.

I held the gun out and surveyed the room. There were

only two other doors in the house. One in the back which led outside, and another to the side where Nadine slept. My niece. That door was closed.

I got to the door and turned the knob. It was locked. I knew Nadine was either dead or taken, but I called out anyway. "Nadine! It's Uncle Garrett. You in there?"

Nothing.

I opened the door, and the sun shot through the window, blinding me, like some kind of blessing, knowing damn well if Nadine was dead, I couldn't bear to see it.

I swung my arm at the air, connected with nothing. I charged into the room and out of the sun's path, finger on the trigger and ready to kill. Nadine was on her bed, legs crossed, eyes wide.

She was alive.

I bent down, put a hand on her knee. "You're safe now, girl." The words held as much weight and comfort as a single grain of sugar on her tongue. It was too late for safety. The damage had been done.

I brought my hand from her knee and saw blood, the source of which came from under her nightie. Her being albino, the blood was like dye on a birch tree. Ink on ivory. Stark and alarming.

I didn't touch her again. I wasn't sure the touch of a man, no matter the intent, would bring solace.

Her left eye was filled with blood and her cheekbone was bruised and swollen. Dirt on her face hung like a mask. The saddest, and maybe scariest, part was the mask held no white streaks where tears should have fallen. She was broken, eyes fixed on the wall behind me like the images of the violent event played over and over again on it, maybe dreaming of a scenario where she murdered those responsible. Or maybe there was no image at all, just a black void.

"I know you don't wanna talk, Nadine. But I need to know who did this to you and your momma."

She tore her eyes from the wall and laid them on me.

That's when the impact hit her. Those ice-pink orbs bubbled over, and the dirt washed away one salty river at a time, then she dove into my arms, and I held her as tight as I could, whispering how sorry I was that I wasn't there when she needed me.

I only ever saw her and her mother every few months, stopping in to do whatever work I could, usually staying a week or so, but this time I ran a day late on account of a bounty I had me a lead on. The reward wasn't a whole lot, but enough to have me saddle up Bones and take a detour. Never did get the bastard.

I didn't expect to ever hear Nadine's voice again. The world don't deserve an angel like her, and if she wanted to crawl inside herself and never come out, I wouldn't blame her. But she did speak.

"It was a man I ain't ever seen before."

"Only one?"

She nodded with her face buried in my shoulder.

"I know you don't want to think about him, but if you can tell me what he looks like just this once, I'll never ask again."

She sat back against the wall and wiped her face. Salty mud streaked sideways. "He had brown eyes."

"Anything else? Was he a fat man, skinny man? Bald?"

"He wasn't skinny or fat, and he had hair. Brown hair, with a dark yellow mustache, 'cept the mustache was kinda crooked."

"Like he slipped while shaving?"

"No, like this part . . . " She put her finger on my mustache, in the middle where the two sides met. "Is over here." Then she moved her finger to the side a little. The man was born with a cleft palate.

"Okay, honey. I know exactly what you mean, and that's everything I need to know. Now, I want you to do your best to forget his face. Every time it pops up, I want you to think of that doll there instead." I pointed toward a rag doll she had sitting on the corner of the bed. Hideous looking thing, but I gathered she saw the beauty in it.

She nodded again, then grabbed the doll.

"Did he say anything? Maybe something to give you an idea on where he was headed?"

She shook her head.

"You stay here. I'll be right back." I stood up to go, and she lunged for me, then doubled over in pain.

"Please don't go, Uncle Garrett." Her voice cracked like a blazing campfire.

I ran my hand over her matted hair, then eased her down on the bed. "I'll just be in the next room. I'm not going anywhere without you. I promise."

She curled up, knees to her chest, and held the ugly doll.

I walked out and scanned the room where my sister poured from her mattress. There were broken dishes on the floor, the table, and one of the chairs was toppled over. She'd given the man a fight.

On the table was some blood—a large smear and a few drops next to that. I reckoned that was his blood, because next to it was a ripped blouse with a long swath of cloth missing from it. He'd made a makeshift bandage for a wound.

I had only glanced at Diane when I first arrived, so I didn't get a look at how brutal it was. Along with her missing nipples, she'd been disemboweled. And he hadn't just stabbed her. Your guts don't spill across the floor like that. He'd pulled them out and played with them.

Other than a glisten deep in the center of her belly, the rest of the blood had dried. I figured she was killed early morning, maybe the night before, though that's not when he would have left. He still had his time with my niece. He would have had to deal with my sister before touching Nadine, cuz ain't no way in hell she would have let that man near her daughter.

Movement caught my eye. Nadine stood at the threshold of her bedroom. "I don't want to stay here no more." Her eyes fell on her mother, following the ropey entrails. I could tell she'd already seen her, maybe even watched it happen.

"You won't have to. We're heading out."

I checked the floor near the fireplace where Diane always kept a gun hidden. There was a loose floorboard there, and inside was a shotgun and a dozen shells, along with a stash of bills and a necklace our mother had given Diane before she died from a broken heart when our pa was killed in a bank robbery. He was the teller at Candlewood National and took a bullet to the head. The thief claimed to have only meant it as a warning shot. If that was true, both men had shit for luck that day.

I put the necklace on Nadine and said, "Go ahead and get yourself cleaned up, then grab the rest of your clothes and anything else you want to bring."

She hobbled away on weak legs. I bent down and kissed my sister's head. A tear threatened to fall, and I denied it.

So she didn't worry, I told Nadine I was heading outside to hook Bones to the wagon. No way the poor girl was able to ride horseback in her condition.

I took what food Diane had and tossed it in the wagon along with as much water as I could carry in my canteen and a few bottles she had lying around, then hitched Diane's horse to the wagon alongside Bones. The two looked good together. Black and white. Yin and Yang, as the Oriental folks sometimes said.

By the time I was done, Nadine was standing at the front door. She looked like a ghost floating there—a dirty white dress with skin that matched Bone's hide. She'd taken shears to her hair, cutting the length just as short as she could. I understood.

"I don't want anyone finding Momma like that," she said, so I went for the barn to get the shovel. "I don't wanna bury her neither."

I turned back. "Well, what'd you have in mind?"

She didn't answer and went back in the house. Within

moments, I saw the warm glow of flames lick the walls inside, and Nadine ran out with nothing but her doll and a blanket. She stood there in the dirt, as though waiting my approval. I nodded, extended my hand. She took it and climbed into the wagon.

I studied the ground for tracks, hoping to find some direction as to where this hare-lipped fucker went. Seeing how it rained twice that week, it wasn't hard. Fortunately, the tracks headed west, toward Franklin's house. Our next stop. If I could get Franklin to come along, this asshole didn't have a chance.

I hopped on the wagon seat, whipped the reins, and we ate the road ahead, while the nightmare burned behind us.

CHAPTER 2

NADINE NEVER ASKED where we were going, never said a word at all that first hour. I looked back a few times, checked on her, thought maybe she found some sleep. But she was sitting upright, gazing at the sky behind us, watching the cloud of smoke made from her mother's charred body and the only home she'd ever known.

Nearly broke down a few times but held back, stuffed that shit inside. It wasn't so much I needed to be strong for the little one. I needed to keep the rage burning. It was fuel, kept my mind on the goal ahead. If I gave up the chase and didn't avenge Nadine and her momma, I'd never forgive myself.

I stopped the wagon long enough to piss and hold Nadine's hand as she went behind a bush. She didn't want me out of her sight, not even for a moment, and I was okay with that. Pain from her lady parts made her wince some while squatting, and I knew she might need to have a doctor look her over once we got to Cross County, where Franklin lived.

I offered her my scarf to clean up, then we headed back to the wagon, her little hand squeezing mine. The grief I felt for her was near unbearable. I was horribly sad my sister was dead—that goes without saying—but my pain didn't compare to Nadine's. Hers was biblical. Sackcloth tearin', head shavin' pain. I never understood those acts of mourning, but I was beginning to. Yet she held her shit together like nothin' I ever seen. Well beyond her years. She'd aged decades on account of a run-in with a madman.

On the way to the wagon, she said, "I stabbed him." Then reached over and touched my right shoulder blade. "Right here."

"You did good, Nadine. And I'm going to do a lot more than stab him when I find the sonofabitch. Ain't no sense in keepin' that secret. You understand?"

She looked at me with those bright pink eyes and gave a hardy nod. "I do, Uncle Garrett." I nearly traded the rage for a river of tears right then and there.

"I suppose we should talk about a few other things while we're at it. I'm not gonna throw honey on my words cuz you're a strong girl, just like your momma. So, I'll be as real with you as I would anyone else. That bein' said, first thing's first. We're family, and I ain't goin' anywhere. Consider them words as solid as those Moses carried down the mount.

"As far as our living situation, we're on the road for now. May be for some time. And you know why. But once done is done, you'll be living at my place. It ain't no mansion, but it's an upgrade. So, now that you're privy, I hope you're not opposed to the plan, cuz it's all I've got."

She stared at the ground as we walked, a slight limp in her gait. "I'm not opposed."

"Was hoping you'd say that."

I helped her back into the wagon, gently. She settled in, then threw her eyes at the horizon—a gorgeous sky that held happiness just out of reach—a sun-shaped carrot-on-a-stick we might never get to.

CHAPTER 3

WE HIT THE outskirts of Cross County where Franklin lived in a shithole shack in a small valley, where all the rain conspired to shoo him out, flooding the tiny house with every big storm.

He didn't live there by choice. It was given to him as the bare minimum after being freed a few years prior. While he got the shack-house, he was robbed of the 40 acres and a mule a lot of other slaves had received. But you'd never hear him complain.

I'd met Franklin when he was still a slave. I used to make deliveries to the Howell plantation he was on. He'd help me unload, and we'd converse about this and that. He had a sense of humor I found both entertaining and enlightening. Despite his circumstances, he wore a smile and often joked about the situation. Once I got to know him, I asked how he managed to make light of being a slave, and he'd said, "There are only two other options, Garrett: lose my mind or kill the whole damn Howell family. Making light keeps my hands off their necks and myself from the gallows."

More than once I nearly brought a hand to Mr. Howell myself on account of how he treated my new friend, but Franklin warned me of the likelihood of losing my job, as well as the fact that any ire would be directed toward him. So, I never touched the man and instead daydreamed about hanging him from my own makeshift gallows, while every slave under his thumb watched.

These days, Franklin spent his quiet days writing, after having been taught to read by one of the house slaves there. His spelling was godawful, but his tales entertaining. That little shack-house was full of stories, written on everything from packaging and birch bark to planks of wood and regular old paper, which I'd grab him whenever the chance.

Franklin greeted us outside as we pulled up. His toothy smile faded when he saw the weight of my face and faded even more when he saw Nadine. He'd met her more than once. I'd brought him with me on a couple visits. He was good with her, and she was fond of him. So was Diane.

"Tell me everything's okay, Garrett." I think my past worry for Diane rubbed off on him. He knew about my concerns—her catching sickness out in the middle of nowhere, or worse yet, some drunken gang showin' up and having their way with her, as these were the times we lived in anymore. Man had traded morality for a strong buzz and a wet hole, even if it meant crossing the line.

"Wish I could."

Franklin ran to the wagon, peeked inside, looking for Diane I figured. "Ahh, hell. What's goin' on?"

I helped Nadine out of the wagon and told her to head on inside and lie down. "We'll be right here talkin'," I said.

She limped on in, and I told Franklin what had transpired.

"What kind of devil does that, Garrett?"

"One that's got a tail chasin' after him, I'll tell you that."

"I'd expect nothin' less. And you'd better believe I'm comin' along."

"Part of the reason I stopped here first."

"Unless you need me watchin' your niece, of course," he said.

"She ain't leaving my side. Appreciate it, though."

"Good. I'd rather get my hands dirty." Franklin stared at the ground a moment, sighed. "Hell . . . Don't even know what to say." He looked at me. "I'm sorry, brother."

"You shoulda seen her, Frank. All pulled apart. Who the fuck slices a woman up like that?"

"A dead man, that's who."

"I wish Nadine hadn't seen her. Now she's gotta live with that image, along with everything else."

Franklin put his hand on my shoulder and squeezed. "We'll find him. The day's early yet. We'll grab some chow and head out, make sure he don't get too far ahead."

"We'd better eat on the way. We're stuck taking the wagon. Ain't no way Nadine can ride horseback. Matter of fact, soon as we hit Cross, I need to get her checked out."

"Enough said. Let me grab my knife and the grub." Franklin didn't own a gun, just one of many things he lived without. Not because he wanted it that way, but, like a lot of newly-freed slaves, he was penniless and mostly unemployed, with the exception of the odd job whenever he could get it. But he had his dignity, and that was more important than even the shithole roof over his head.

"Hold on. I got you a gun." I grabbed Diane's shotgun from the wagon, along with the shells, and handed them over.

Franklin took the gun in his hands like it was a newborn baby. "This Diane's?"

I nodded.

"You sure you wanna part with it?"

"Hell yes. I've got my rifle and six-shooter. That's all I need. Now get that grub, and a pen. Maybe the hunt will pull a story out of you."

Franklin set his gun under the wagon's bench and made for the house. A few minutes later we were headed toward Cross County.

CHAPTER 4

FRANKLIN'S SHACK-HOUSE was far enough away from Cross to burn down in the middle of the night without seeing the glow from there, but close enough to consider him a citizen.

It was a pleasant enough town, even to the black folks, but nobody had offered Franklin steady work. Thankfully, he'd managed to win enough hearts over to be the go-to guy when something laborious needed doing.

While the population was small, it still held all the makings of a town born to flourish—a general store, saloon, stables, post office, doctor's office, and a sheriff's station. The necessities, while not busy just yet, were built early on to attract citizens, presenting the impression that this wasn't just another village in the middle of nowhere.

Probably its most unique, albeit bizarre, attraction was the zoo, complete with two wooden sculptures at the entrance depicting what I assumed were tigers, though resembled gargoyles more than any big cat.

I'd only ever seen the zoo from afar and always thought the town had no business having one. Not with our climate. I wasn't even sure what creatures were caged inside, but you could hear all sorts of howls, growls, and chirps coming from within those walls.

As we passed by, I pointed out the sculptures to Nadine. Figured if she liked that hideous doll, she just might like the gargoyle-tigers. She did.

With no time to mess around, we headed straight for

the doctor's—Mr. Greenfield. I met him once or twice. A short, timid fellow with glasses too big for his boyish face. Greenfield was always reading them adventure books like they was the gospel and he was on his deathbed. I never did understand anyone who spent that much time staring at words when there's a whole world moving right in front of them. Hell, go to the zoo. But that was the doctor. If he was awake, and his fingers weren't pluckin' a bullet from a leg, his nose was buried in pages.

I held Nadine's hand as we went in. Franklin followed. He found out a long time ago that sitting in a wagon by himself could attract the wrong type. The next thing you know he's throwing punches just to stop from being killed. Course, nobody ever blamed the white man for a scuffle. That blame fell on Franklin. Always.

The doc's place was nice. Clean. If the color white had a smell, his office reeked of it. Greenfield sat at a desk in the center of a small room, face in book, and looked up over his too-big glasses with a smile. We'd made his day. Didn't matter what the problem was, we were customers.

"Dr. Greenfield. This here's my good friend Franklin. Not sure you two have met. He lives down the road. Helpful man. Real good man."

Franklin elbowed me in the side. I had a habit of singing his praises whenever the chance. It was real bad, almost like I was a traveling salesman, selling my friend's good-spirited heart, and it didn't usually dawn on me until the words were out of my mouth. If Franklin hadn't brought it to my attention I would have gone on.

"And this here's my niece, Nadine. Now, her I don't believe you've met."

"Hello, Franklin. Nadine." He nodded and came around the desk. He had a good bedside manner, like even just coming from around that desk made me feel like we was all in this together and he wasn't just a businessman providing a service. "What can I do for ya?"

I turned to Nadine. "Give me one minute, honey." I

looked at Franklin. He nodded, and I directed Dr. Greenfield toward the back, where I'd sat once while he looked at my throat, checking it for spots. Not even sure what the spots meant, but turns out I didn't have them, just a sore throat from sleeping with my mouth open.

The room back there was even cleaner than the office. Made me wonder just how much death and disease the place had seen. I didn't figure much.

"Doc . . . this is a sensitive subject, and I need to know you're gonna treat it as such."

"I'm a professional, Mr. Walkinshaw. I didn't go to school to run a war-tent clinic. In case you haven't noticed, I've got a nice place here—"

"That's part of my worry. I could eat off these floors. They don't exactly scream experience if you know what I mean."

"Get to the point, Walkinshaw." I'd hit a nerve. Didn't blame him.

"My niece. She's been raped, and I don't know what that does to a young girl. I just know she was bleeding and she's in pain, and I need you to look her over, which I imagine she's not gonna be too fond of."

I could tell by the way his face melted he now understood my concern about professionalism and sensitivity.

"Holy hell . . . " was all he said for a moment, his eyes searching mine. "Of course, Garrett. And I'd like you to be present. We'll want to make her as comfortable as possible. And may I just say, I'm sorry. I don't know the details, but I'm sure the law will find the man responsible, if they haven't already, and justice will be served."

"It most certainly will."

He cocked his head like a dog who'd heard a whistle, as though asking if I meant to take things into my own hands. But I think he knew the answer.

"I'll get Nadine."

I brought Nadine to the room and told her the doctor

was gonna check her over, make sure she was okay. I said, "You're not gonna like this, but you need to be strong and let the doctor do what he does."

I didn't like bringing a stranger into Nadine's business. But all the blood, and the way she limped. For all I knew, the man had cut her up down there, which seemed feasible considering what he'd done to Diane.

Nadine held my hand tight, and I talked about my ranch and the buffalo that roam the fields, and that one time I saw an actual camel, which had me thinkin' I'd lost my mind or had been slipped mescaline until I heard about the U.S. Army bringing them over to Texas—someone's bright idea of a proper mount during the war—and a few still wandered like ghosts on the plains. I thought of everything I could just to keep her mind off the doc and how close he was to parts that no man but her husband should be privy to.

After Dr. Greenfield was done, he told us that she had a tear but it was not to the degree she'd need stitching. He offered them anyway, stating he had some top-of-the-line catgut sutures that'd come sterilized, but Nadine said she'd rather it heal on its own, which was the other option.

"Keep the area clean, and don't run. As far as the pain goes, that should leave with time. And if it doesn't, or seems to get worse, come back and see me. I'd also like you to keep an eye out for any sores or rashes. You see any of those, you come see me right away. We can't rule out syphilis just yet."

"Well, when I find the hare-lipped asshole I'll have to personally ask about his medical history. Thank you kindly, Dr. Greenfield."

Greenfield reached out, grabbed my arm. "Did you say harelip?"

"Yes . . . or whatever the hell the medical term is."

"Did the harelipped gentlemen happen to have a knife wound?"

The question knocked the wind out of me, and out of

the corner of my eye I saw Nadine fidget. If I had the ears of a dog, I figured I could hear her heart picking up pace. "Matter of fact, he did."

"On his right shoulder blade?"

"Yep. You saw him?"

"He left my office not four hours ago. Stitched him up, and he headed out."

"He say anything about where he was headed?"

"He did ask how far away Branchwood was. Other than that, barely spoke a word. He refused anesthetic, wouldn't even take a shot of whiskey. I had a feeling about the man when he stepped foot in here. Now I know I was right." He looked at Nadine. "Always trust your gut, sweetheart."

I asked the man for a description. He said the same things Nadine had said: Headful of brown hair with eyes to match, dark-yellow mustache, no hat, medium build, harelip. "He didn't smell so good either. Not your typical odor from a man who needs to bathe, but something bittersweet, almost rotten."

"Thank you, Dr. Greenfield. What do I owe you?" I reached for my money, started counting. He gave me a price I thought was fair, and I paid the man.

"I'd go straight to Sheriff Chivers. Just keep heading into town, and you can't miss the building. Big star painted on the front. If you need my testimony I'd be happy to come down and give it. Just let me know if I'm needed."

The doc knew I had no intention of getting the law involved, so I'm not sure why he wasted his time. For his own conscience, I suppose.

"Thanks, Doc. I'll do just that."

He gave me a knowing side eye, and I helped Nadine back to the main office where Franklin was waiting, then we all headed outside to the wagon.

As I was telling Franklin we was on the right track, someone screamed from down the road. Another scream joined the first. Then another.

A chain reaction of horror. I looked toward the zoo and

saw people running in different directions, like ants on fire. The loudest scream seemed to be coming from a gentleman whose silhouette appeared disproportionate, like his arms were too long for his body, then for a minute, I thought maybe that wasn't a man at all but a monkey, dragging its knuckles in the dirt behind it. But as the figure got closer, running toward us, I noticed it was a man after all. His white shirt was stained with blood up toward the shoulders, while his arms were indeed dangling behind him, bouncing off the road like two dead men tied to a fleeing horse.

I saw men all around free pistols from their sides and take aim, so I told Nadine to get in the wagon and pulled my own gun. Franklin ran for his.

I heard a growl and put the pieces together. This town what had a boner for caging animals and exploitin' them for tourists, well, that ill-planned idea came back to bite them in the most literal sense of the word. Not a second went by before my thoughts were confirmed, and I finally saw the beast what ripped the man's arms from his body. It was a gorgeous thing, graceful in it its step and fearful in its roar. The tiger reared its head and let out the most intimidating sound I'd ever heard, baring its teeth at the running crowd around it.

The doc ran out of his office and stood there, taking it in, mouth agape. The man with the dangling arms was running straight for him, and after one more good bounce off the road, his left arm fell off and sat there in the middle of the road waiting to be buried.

Guns went off and bullets flew, and I saw a silhouette drop in the street like a sack of potatoes. It seemed to me some of the shooters had all the aim of a man halfway through his second bottle, and suddenly it wasn't the tiger I was afraid of.

I hopped on the wagon seat and grabbed the reins, while Franklin got the same idea and joined me.

I heard another roar and saw the tiger take a swing at

a shooter, hooking the side of the man's face. Bits sailed through the air I imagined were probably teeth. Then another gun fired, and another body dropped.

I snapped the reins, and we raced from the scene, kicking up a wall of dust that blocked the continuing carnage from our view. Even when the gunfire finally died down, and the screams were stuffed with cotton, we kept on riding, hoping the trail we were on would lead us to redemption.

CHAPTER 5

THE HORSES WERE TIRED, so we took advantage of a small creek Franklin spotted just off the road. We stretched our legs, ate, drank, and Nadine said a few words for the poor tiger who was most likely dead, or on the loose and would wind up with its ribs drying in the sun soon enough.

As Nadine spoke, I felt bad that not only did my sister not get a proper burial, but no words were said on her behalf. Then, as though Nadine had read my thoughts, she spoke of her mother, going on about God and mercy and forgiveness and Heaven. I held back tears again. There'd come a day for weeping, but the way I saw it, Diane would rather have us riding the ass of the man who did this than mope and lose our will to do anything at all.

While riding toward the next town, offering my own words to God about the absolute need for finding the madman we were after, we came across a wagon on the side of the road. Passing on by was the initial plan, but after it looked to be abandoned, we stopped.

Franklin and I quickly spoke about the danger—and foolishness—of stopping, as this was an old trick thieves used, even with trains. Some assholes in waiting would lay the bait and a good Samaritan would take it. But since there were no trees or bushes to hide behind and nothing but flatland that stretched as far as we could see, we stopped. There was a chance someone really did need help.

Also, since we had reason to believe the man we were

looking for headed this way, I had a bad feeling he'd left his mark here.

We grabbed our guns, and I instructed Nadine to lie down in the back, hide under a blanket, and not so much as peek our way until I gave the go ahead.

We checked the wagon, and it was empty, save for a modest amount of provisions and a rifle. But when Franklin pointed toward the tall grass just a short distance away, before I even followed his finger, I knew what I'd find. The bright red blood against the pale-yellow grass was a surreal sight. It certainly didn't belong. I scanned the area. Still no place to hide for anyone who meant harm, unless of course the body in the field was mocking death, waiting until we drew close so they could pounce, take our goods, and leave us stranded.

But they was dead all right. The woman looked much the same way Diane did. Breasts exposed, nipples taken. Her guts weren't spread out like my sister's had been, but this woman's face was gone, peeled right off with nothing left but an angry-red shine made of muscle, a skeleton smile, and two wide eyes staring at the sky, dried and sunken like a fish on the shore during summer.

"Well . . ." Franklin muttered. "Looks like we're on the right track."

My thoughts exactly.

Further off the road was another body. This one was a man. He was shirtless, and his hands had been cut off at the wrists, his arms like two fleshy posts that tapered at the end, dipped in raspberry jam. Whoever was doing this was one sick bastard, with no intent to stop. They were getting off on it.

I turned around and saw Nadine peeking her head out. She saw me, and instead of hiding, got out and headed straight for the abandoned wagon, then climbed inside.

"Nadine!" I ran toward her. "I told you to stay hidden. It ain't safe for you out here."

She jumped out of the empty wagon with a rifle in her hand, winced when she landed.

"Nadine . . . I need you to listen when I—"

"I need a gun, Uncle Garrett." She cocked the thing, checked the chamber. "You'd be right to let me carry one. None of us are safe." Then she went back in the wagon to search for bullets.

"You ain't but eleven years old. Far too young to be totin' a weapon like that."

She stuck her head out. "I've been shootin' since I was five. Is it cuz I'm a woman?" Her face scrunched against the sun, and she gave me an irritated eye.

"First off . . . you ain't no woman. You're a girl. And yes, I suppose that's part of it."

I could hear the clink of bullets in her hand as she found a box of them. "So, you think girls can't shoot?" She climbed down from the wagon.

"You can use Franklin's knife, how about that? You seem to be proficient with one."

She ignored me and threw a bullet in the rifle, raised it, barely aimed at something I couldn't see, then pulled the trigger. The gun rang out like thunder, and I swung my head in the direction she'd aimed, just in time to see a large bird hit the ground.

"Damn!" Franklin said as he met up with us. "I sure as shit can't shoot like that."

"If something happens where you can't protect me, I need to be able to do it myself, Uncle Garrett."

I looked at her. Hair chopped, laugh lines I suspect weren't from laughing at all but squinting in the sun while working on her momma's ranch. She was hardened, and I could tell that hare-lipped fella would be the last man she ever took shit from again.

"Alright. Just don't be shootin' at everything you see."

She nodded, then climbed in the back of our wagon. "We should grab the food they had. They won't be needing it."

Nadine had changed. I figured all that time to reflect in the wagon, bouncing in the back as she gazed at the sky, she came to some conclusions—one of them that she was done being a victim and was ready to put a bullet in the madman just as much as Franklin and myself. Like shedding skin, the little girl in her had gone away, and I got to wondering if the word "woman" didn't fit her more aptly now. Then, as we rode down the trail toward Branchwood, all was clarified as I caught sight of that ugly doll being thrown from the wagon and into the tall grass.

CHAPTER 6

AS WE RODE WEST, I began to wonder if I ever really knew Nadine at all. That maybe because I wasn't around much I had this preconceived notion—an 11-year-old girl who wore dresses, played with dolls, and dreamt of nothing more than being taken care of by a strong, handsome man one day.

Then, I started to realize the tough and rough of her had been there well before her momma was killed. It was something taught by her mom. Self-preservation, survival, and independence. Diane knew it was a man's world, and if you let him, he'd keep on reminding you of such. Their run-in with the madman had validated every warning she ever gave her daughter. And now here we were, hunting him down with the intent to kill, and Nadine was ready, like she'd trained for this battle, throwing on her armor through those short eleven years, one piece at a time. There was no taming her. Too late for that. And words of warning from my mouth were nothing but a whistle in the wind, any leash I'd try and use would be broken from. It made me both nervous and proud.

The heat bore down with a weight you could feel, pressing our shoulders toward our knees and coating our skin with a shine like we'd passed through rain. I was thankful for the cover. It kept Nadine in the shade, and later in the day, once the sun swung behind us, we could sit in its shadow up front. To pass the time, Franklin struck up a conversation, told Nadine about his slave days.

"How's come some were allowed in the house and some weren't?" she asked him.

"That's a fair question, Nadine. One I asked myself every night. But inside or out, we was all still slaves."

"Did the house slaves eat the same food?"

"No ma'am they did not."

There was silence from Nadine for a moment. Then, "It seems to me because you worked the hardest, out in the sun and all, you shoulda been the one inside, eating the other food and sleeping in a real bed."

"I tend to agree. But those in the house never saw what they had as a blessing because weren't none of it a blessing. They wasn't free, just like we wasn't free in the fields. We all suffered. Together."

"That's admirable."

"That's a mighty big word, Ms. Nadine," Franklin chuckled.

"You ever think about going back and getting revenge?" she asked.

Franklin looked at me. "No, I don't. Because now I'm full of blessings, and I wouldn't wanna do anything that might take them away. What's done is done. Those was bad days, but they're gone."

"Well . . . if what's done is done, then why are we chasing the man who did this to me and Momma?"

Franklin and I traded glances again, searching each other for a good enough answer to give that wasn't full of hypocrisy.

"Cuz if we don't, then he'll keep on killing," I said.

Nadine's questions stopped, and she seemed to consider the answer, grabbing an apple and filling her mouth with it.

"She ain't no dummy," Franklin whispered, then ran a prideful hand over the shotgun in his lap, polishing the wood with his shirt. It was my hope he'd never have to use the thing, and I worried about him nearly as much as I had worried about Diane. Blacks had a target on their backs too. Not everyone was happy they'd acquired the freedom they had.

When Franklin was first granted freedom, I'd asked him to come stay with me, but he wasn't having it. Independence was important to him, so was dignity. Or maybe it was pride disguised as such. Either way, I respected his choice to live in the shithole shack and did my best to put myself in his boots, figuring I'd probably do the same. I don't think I'd want another man taking care of me, making sure I was kept safe. I'd begin to not feel like a person anymore, and since that's probably exactly how Franklin felt every year he was at the Howell plantation, even living in a dump like the shack helped bring the dignity back that every man needed.

Diane was like that too, and it seemed so was Nadine. There'd come a day before too long where she'd want nothing to do with being taken care of, not even by a man who'd take her as his bride. And it scared the hell out of me to think about.

CHAPTER 7

SADDLED HORSES ROAMED the field ahead, and just beyond that was a house and stable off the road. If our prey stayed on this trail, it would be the first house he'd come across. And with the unmanned horses on the loose, it didn't look good.

We stopped in front of the house. All three of us grabbed our guns and climbed down. Recent rains hadn't touched the land this far west, so the ground coughed dust around our feet, searching for skin to coat and a pair of lungs to dwell in.

Until that moment, I hadn't gotten a good look at Nadine's gun. It was a model I hadn't seen before. Brand new and looked as though it cost more than I'd ever spend, but envy didn't cross my mind. If any of us needed a reliable gun that had true sight, it was Nadine.

I stepped in front of her and gently pushed her behind me. I'd already explained that no young girl should ever find herself in the middle of a shootout, or be witness to the carnage we were likely to see—even tried reminding her of doctor's orders and that staying off her feet might be best. But, since she ignored my request to stay hidden, I wanted to make sure if a bullet flew from inside the house it'd likely hit me first.

A gust of wind threw the stable door open and whistled through the gapped planks like a banshee. All manner of tools and buckets lay abandoned across the ground, and there was a dark-red handprint smeared on the door.

"Hello?" The wind ate my words as I crept toward the door, rifle at my hip.

"Anyone in there?" Franklin called out next to me.

There was no reply. Franklin rushed the door and opened it. Flies buzzed, and a wall of odor hit us. The body hadn't been there long. The smell was mostly a dead man's last meal. The same smell that sprouts at the gallows when the hanged fill their pants.

Bent face down on the table was a man stripped naked, deep grooves carved down his arms and legs like the red-stitched seams on a life-sized doll. Crusted shit trailed down his legs and sat in a pile on the floor.

I quickly turned and faced Nadine, grabbed her by the shoulders and led her back to the wagon. Franklin followed.

"This is a hell of a trail he's leaving." he said.

"Ain't ever seen anything like it."

"He have any parts missing?" Nadine said, just one of the guys now it seemed. She laid her gun in the back under a blanket, then climbed in and got comfortable.

"I don't know and don't care to find out," I said.

"You know . . . " Franklin set his gun under the bench. "I get that you want revenge by your hands. I do too. But I wouldn't be against sharing what we know with the law if it means the killin' stops sooner than later."

"Was thinking the same thing. Branchwood is just ahead. We'll fill them in."

Franklin squinted, eyes fixed on something behind me. "Looks like we might have our chance right now."

I turned and saw three men riding on horses, badges on their chests that twinkled in the sun like their own warm greeting. While they took their time riding up, I tossed my rifle in the wagon with Franklin's and grabbed a few apples for the horses. Bones lost his appetite and got twitchy as the men approached. It was a bad sign.

"Afternoon," I said, my hand petting Bones to keep him calm.

The lawmen said nothing at first, just looked me over, then Franklin. Their eyes stayed on him for an uncomfortable amount of time, like his face was made of words meant to read.

"What are you boys doing 'round here at Carlton's?" The man who said this wore a sheriff's badge. He was the biggest of the three, and I don't mean tall. This guy hadn't ever skipped a meal. The black wisps of hair he still had laid across his head like a spider's legs.

"If Carlton is the man who lives here, I think you need to take a look inside," I said.

"Is that so?" Another guy said. He was thin and weathered like an old leather glove left in the sun, or a saddle that'd seen too much ass. The top of his head was much like the sheriff's, except the wisps were blonde and danced in the wind like they were trying to make a run for it. The rest of his hair hung darn near to his shoulders.

"The man inside is dead," Franklin said. The lawmen gave him another once over.

"If that's true, things don't look too good for you, nigger." The third man said this. He was a handsome fella who I imagine was probably popular with the ladies back home but looked too young to be deputized, yet he wore a deputy's badge that matched Leather Man's.

I felt a storm coming with these men and did my best to part the clouds. "Now, hold on, fellas. We've been tracking a murderer since morning. Me and my real good friend Franklin here. And so far, the man has killed four people, your friend inside included. I brought Franklin along with me because not only is he the most loyal and trusting man you'll ever meet, if something needs doing, he's the one you call on."

"Is that so?" It seemed those three words were the only ones Leather Man knew.

While the men dismounted, I caught Nadine out of the corner of my eye. She was peeking over the wagon seat, her rifle aimed straight at the Sheriff and his men. I mouthed for her to get down, and to my surprise, she did. When I looked back at the lawmen, they had their guns drawn, and Franklin had his hands up.

"Now, for safety's sake, how about you two lead the way," the Sheriff said as he tugged on his belt with his free hand, tucking his gut in.

"Not a problem," I said, then walked to the front door and opened it.

The sound of flies and the smell of shit seemed to set the deputies off, and as they raised their guns like they meant to shoot, I got the impression they ain't ever run across anything like this either. They were scared.

"Head on in," the Sheriff waved his gun toward the door. His demeanor was calm, almost too calm, like he had some plans beyond that door.

I wanted to look back, make sure Nadine was staying put, but didn't dare draw attention to her. Instead, I prayed she was smart enough not to fire that rifle, particularly at three men sporting badges.

Franklin and I walked in, stood to the side, and looked at the poor bastard bent over the table. Shit, blood, and split skin. The sheriff came in after us, then the deputies. One deputy covered his nose, the other his mouth.

The sheriff puffed his chest out to meet his belly and said, "Nope. This don't look good at all." Then aimed his gun at Franklin's head. "You wanna tell me what happened here?"

"Like my friend said, we was—"

"Shut up, nigger. I ain't talking to you." He kept eyes on Franklin but it seemed he was talking to me. "Again . . . you wanna tell me what happened here?"

I told him about finding my sister—though I left Nadine out of it—and how I met up with Franklin cuz he's the best damn person I know, and about the people off the side of the road and now Carlton here.

"You said if something needs done that your friend here is the adequate man for the job," Leather Man said.

"That's right. You won't find none better."

"In that case, looks to me like Carlton could use a bath. We can't very well let his family see him like this."

Not to say every man with a badge was an honest one, but I got the feeling these weren't lawmen at all and nothing more than troublemaking bandits who stumbled across their stars somehow. I called them on it.

"Your mouth don't match your badge, deputy."

He hit me a good one across the face, splitting my lip with the butt of his gun. I stumbled back against the wall, collected the blood in my mouth, and spat it on the ground.

The sheriff let out a quick chuckle, and the young guy said to Franklin, "You heard the deputy, boy. Clean that shit up."

"With your tongue," Leather Man said.

Young Guy recoiled, scrunched his face. "Yeah . . . lick them legs clean, nigger."

I could see the anger in Franklin's face, the clench of his fists, and knew he was debating on dying with dignity or appeasing those who just might kill us all. His days of humiliation should have been over years ago—should have never been anyhow—but here he was dealing with the same kind of bullshit he had most of his life. But I knew Franklin enough to know his dignity didn't come from rebellion but from being humble and from being wise, and if I didn't stop this nonsense he'd be on his knees licking the shit off a dead man's legs.

Me on the other hand, my dignity came from a place of ignorance and pride.

"Sheriff. You tell your kids to sink them guns into leather and shut the fuck up, or I'll shove 'em up their assholes."

The last thing I remember is seeing the butt of that gun again.

CHAPTER 8

IT WAS NADINE what woke me up. Crying, tugging on my shoulders. I opened my eyes. May as well have been underwater. I sat up, and my head pulsated with the rage of a thousand mornings after. I was in dire need of some laudanum to kill the pain.

"Uncle Garrett!" Nadine's voice was a distant hum that eventually registered after calling out a few more times. "Uncle Garrett! We have to get Franklin."

The hazy image of a too-pale, short-haired girl in a dress appeared before me, and I remembered everything. "They take him?"

"Yeah. I'm sorry, Uncle Garrett. I wanted to shoot, but there was three of them and—"

"You did good, Nadine. You did the right thing. Had you taken a shot, we'd all have a halo of flies right now."

"Let's go." She grabbed my hand and pulled it hard, rushed me toward the door. My head pounded harder, and I dropped to my knees.

I held my hand up, telling her to just hold on a second. Let me get a sense of things, like how to walk without pukin'. "First thing's first." I rubbed my head and felt a good-sized lump there. "We're gonna have to hit Branchwood. I don't think those men were of the law, so we'll have to ask around, see if we can't find their whereabouts."

"They are the law. And I know where they are. When I was hiding in the wagon like you told me, I heard everything they said. See that smoke over there?" She pointed through the pasture and up a slight incline where a forest sat. A line of smoke shot up from somewhere deep in the woods. "That's where their base is. That's what they kept calling it. Their base. And they're fittin' to make Franklin a slave again."

I was glad to hear they spilled enough to clue Nadine in, but hearing they really was the law put spiders in my gut. Killing a man cuz he's a murdering piece of shit was one thing, but going after lawmen with the intent on digging them a grave was something altogether different.

I glanced over at the dead man on the table and took note of the pale-white stripes that ran down his legs where shit and blood once mixed in dark rivers. I wish I hadn't seen that.

"They take the wagon and the guns?"

"They left 'em . . . but they killed Bones and Naddy."

Nadine had named her mother's horse after herself, ridden countless miles in the pasture behind their house, and cared for the beast her whole life—fed, brushed, and spent time with it as one would a friend. While the death of Bones upset me, Naddy hit me harder. Just another loss for poor Nadine.

With a dizzy head, I stood and ran outside, stumbling. Bones lay with his legs crumpled under him like matchsticks, his throat split with a wide gash. Naddy lay in the road on her side, having left a trail of crimson behind her.

"Fucking monsters," I said, then apologized to Nadine for the vulgarity.

"It's what they are."

We grabbed as many provisions out of the wagon as we could comfortably carry, as well as our guns—Nadine's rifle and both my pistol and my rifle.

I spotted a silhouette in the road up ahead, the very same spot we first saw the lawmen. It was another rider. He was by himself, and the way his head struggled to balance on his shoulders I figured he was a few drinks in.

"Keep your gun at the ready," I told Nadine, though I don't think I had to.

"Howdy, stranger," the man said.

I nodded.

"You here for the meeting? Samson said he was bringin' on some new blood. That must be you."

I played along. "Yep. Looks like he's runnin' late, though."

The man laughed. "Most likely waitin' on them dicknuts of his."

"Most likely."

The man stayed on his horse, slouched. "He mention anything to you about who we're hittin' tonight?"

"Not to me. I figure that's what the meeting's for." I was starting to get an idea on what this gang of jackasses was all about.

He looked at Nadine, seemed to take notice of her for the first time. "Holy hell, sweetheart. You glow like the moon. Ain't no confusin' you with a coon, that's for damn sure."

"So, about tonight," I said. "Who do you think we're . . . hitting?"

He looked back at me. "I been talkin' up them niggers over near the Boden farm for months now. If I had to guess, I'd say them. Family of four. Fuckin' moon crickets don't know how to—"

Before he finished the sentence, I drew my revolver and put a bullet in the fucker's chest. He flew back over his horse's ass, and a moment later I heard the pop of his neck as the top of his head met the ground, snapping his teeth shut and biting the end of his tongue clean off.

As the dust settled around the man's body, I told Nadine I was sorry she had to see that.

"I'm not," was all she said, then scurried over to him, searching for money and bullets, then to the horse. When she pulled a white sheet from his saddlebag, my suspicions were confirmed. And I realized Franklin was in a hell of a lot more trouble than I thought.

CHAPTER 9

NADINE AND I argued about whether or not to take the horse. Due to her condition, I insisted we walk. But her point on walking the distance being more harmful for her than riding won the debate, though I suspect even if she had no point at all, she'd have put up a fight just to get to Franklin sooner. Even if riding meant opening a wound that was trying to heal.

Considering Carlton's place seemed to be the popular go-to, we decided it'd be best to leave for the woods right away. Just before we left, I heard the man on the ground let out a wheeze that made me wonder if he was alive. I'd heard about dead men making noises with gas and whatnot, but to be sure, I rode his own horse over him a few times. The horse had no qualms about being careful with its step, and if the man was still breathin', he wasn't anymore.

As we raced through the pasture, Nadine held tight to my waist. Every once in a while, I'd hear her grunt and ask if she was okay until she found herself irritated and demand I keep quiet about it.

I took careful note of that smoke and picked a spot in the trees up ahead where we'd enter, making as straight a shot as we could through the forest with the hopes of not veering off and bypassing the base altogether. Before long, we were too close to the trees to see the smoke, and we stopped at the forest edge next to a giant Bur Oak.

We got off the horse and let her go. No sense in tying

her up and leaving her for dead. I knew eventually we'd either be stealing the horses what belonged to the law, or never walk out of that forest again.

The woods were thick, making it difficult to walk a straight line. We took careful steps, dodging dead branches that may snap underfoot. In my head, I was like an Indian—a silent ghost on his way to a kill. But in reality, my effort was laughable and inadequate. Regardless of my attention to the ground and its surroundings, I was like a drunk on his way to bed across a loose wooden floor topped with marbles. Nadine's steps, however, were feathers on a cloud, despite the pain between her legs.

We walked that way for what must have been an hour until I heard a sound behind us and to the right. We froze. Listened. Then I heard a cackle off in the distance along with the low rumble of a man's voice.

We turned around and headed toward the voice, moving slower than before. Up ahead, I could see a structure what looked like a cabin, then wisps of gray trailing up through the trees—a campfire. Sure enough, we'd passed the base.

As we crept closer, I debated on whether or not to wait until dark before heading in. The night would hide us, but we'd be stumbling blindly through an area we weren't familiar with, so I decided using the thick foliage to our advantage was our best bet.

Once we were on the border of what looked like their property, we crouched down and scanned the base. There were two buildings identical to one another, both of which looked as though they'd been built by children, hit by a train, then reassembled during a windstorm. Between them, and closer to us, was a small shack that looked like the builders had learned a thing or two after their first two attempts. Next to that was a long woodpile and a stump with an ax jutting from it. I could make out a stable further in, past the two buildings, which wasn't much more than a lean-two, as well as what I assumed was an outhouse. In the center of it all was a dirt clearing surrounded by log benches with a firepit in the middle. On two of the benches were the deputies.

Nadine pointed something out I hadn't seen. Next to the outhouse was a black man hanging by his neck, wearing nothing but an old shirt covered in dark stains. It wasn't Franklin, but I knew it would be if we didn't get to him soon.

I ducked behind the tree and sat down, wiped sweat and worry from my brow. "I'll be honest with you, Nadine . . . as I always have and always will. I don't know the first thing about raising a kid, let alone a girl. But what I do know is those men over there don't deserve the air they breathe, and if we walk away now then we don't deserve that air neither."

"Ain't no other way, Uncle Garrett. I know that."

"Yeah, I suppose you do. I'm just . . . covering my ass here, I guess. But I reckon you're wiser than I give you credit for."

I wanted to tell her not to let this kinda bullshit stop her from being the woman she may have dreamt about being, not to let her scars shape her. But in that moment, I needed her strong and focused, so I put that conversation in the back of my mind for another time, when we wasn't facing a kill-or-be-killed situation.

As Nadine and I hid behind a large enough tree to hide us both while sitting, I cleared away the ground and drew a map of the base in the dirt, using pebbles and broken sticks to represent pertinent landmarks like the two buildings, the shack, outhouse, stable, and woodpile. Using the map, I planned a route to take while she covered me. I'd only ever seen her shoot one bullet, but it hit its target, and I could tell she was sharp enough to rely on from afar.

"There's a good chance I'll break from this route on account of them being unpredictable," I told her. "But these landmarks here are the best cover I've got, so if I'm not hiding behind any of them, I'm likely dead. Your job is to keep your eyes on them and not me. You see I've gotten someone's attention, that's the one you take down."

Her pink eyes were fixed on me, intent on retaining every word like it was gospel.

"See that tree with the broken limb?" I pointed forward some 100 feet or so. "You take cover behind it while I move in. I'll follow the route best I can. I figure the sheriff is somewhere inside, maybe more of 'em too. But let's focus on the deputies. Keep in mind, that first shot rings out, the whole camp will come a runnin', so wait for my signal. Unless they spot me before then. In that case, start shooting."

She took a deep breath and closed her eyes, like maybe she was praying, then looked at me and nodded that she understood and was ready.

We crawled to the tree with the broken limb, I nodded, then went left and crept through the brush and toward the outhouse. I looked back to see Nadine had her sight on the deputies, ready to fire.

As I got close to the outhouse, the dangling dead man became a distraction. He looked a lot like Franklin—built like a rock and tall with a thick neck. Or maybe that was swelling. Death does strange things to a body. Either way, it was easy to picture my best friend up there with his eyes bugged out, and I had a mind to storm the bastards right then, lose my shit and start shooting.

But then I heard a man grunt in the outhouse, and I froze.

CHAPTER 10

WHEN FRANKLIN LEFT the Howell plantation, that first day as a free man, he walked to my house—nearly 30 miles in shoes that were better for wipin' your ass than they was for walking.

He showed up with two black eyes, a split lip, and a limp. I asked him what had happened, and he said, "All that matters is I'm a free man now, and I'm here to see ya." But I knew he'd crossed the path of evil men on his way. But that's Franklin for you, always lookin' at the brighter side of life. A real optimist. If he had no food to call his own, he'd give glory to God for eyes to see the food he was missin'. Being locked up somewhere in that camp, I wasn't sure what was on his mind. If he'd just given up, broken down after having had his freedom stripped. Or holding out hope and thanking God he still had legs, even if they was chained. I needed to be that hope for him. And that's what kept me going toward the shitter with the grunter inside.

With the poor soul hanging overhead, and the smell of fresh shit in my nose, I waited behind the outhouse. There was a good chance the deputies could see me once I stepped out from behind the structure, but I had to take that chance. If the sheriff was the grunter, I'd rather deal with him now than have him taking cover inside one of them buildings, shooting at us through the dark windows. Problem was, I didn't have a knife to quietly stick him. Not even something to beat him on the head with, 'cept my gun.

My luck, that'd go off after a swing or two. So, the way I saw it, I had two options: do my best to drag him behind the outhouse without the deputies seeing—this was a helluva longshot—or shoot the grunter in the back, then fire quick as I could toward the campfire. I'm no marksman, so I counted on that one missing, hoping Nadine would make up for it.

Either the man inside had squirts that wouldn't quit or a log that wouldn't roll, because I crouched behind the outhouse, smelling his ass and the dead man above for longer than I liked. Ten minutes went by, and the grunts and the moans and sighs continued, until finally I heard the creak of wood and the clanging of a belt. I looked around for the seventh time, searching for a large rock or a log I could use instead of the bullet, but God still hadn't dropped one for me. I'd have to shoot the man and draw all eyes on me.

I looked at Nadine, her eyes darting between me and the deputies. I heard the door latch, and I came out from behind the outhouse, rifle raised. I looked to Nadine again and gave the signal. The grunter inside walked out, took two steps toward the campfire—which lay some 40 feet ahead. It wasn't the sheriff. That meant there were at least four of them.

Before I got a chance to pull the trigger, the grunter called out, dragging the deputies' attention straight at me. "You assholes said them beans was still good. I just shit my brains—"

I pulled the trigger, and the bullet found the back of the man's skull. Blood sprayed out the front like he'd spat it from a snuff-filled mouth. By the time his body met the dust, Leather Man had grabbed his own neck where Nadine put a hole in it.

The young deputy fumbled for his revolver, and I pulled the trigger once more. Missed. He found his gun and shot toward me. I ducked behind the outhouse, and the bullet hit wood. I heard Nadine fire again. She must have missed too because the deputy kept unloading. I peeked out from the other side of the outhouse and fired another round. This one hit his shin, and he fell forward into the fire, hands out in front of him. Sparks flew and nightmarish screams ripped through the trees.

Glass shattered, and I heard another shot, this time from one of those dark windows I was so afraid of. The sheriff or another minion, I wasn't sure. Until I heard him cussing about his losses. "You cocksuckin' bitches!"

The man on fire flailed about, running, spinning, kicking dust. I ain't ever heard a man scream like that before and hope I never will again. Finally, after tripping over one of the log benches, he fell. His head bounced off the ground, and the screaming stopped.

Another shot rang out. It seemed to me the sheriff was shooting at Nadine. I couldn't just sit there and hide behind the shitter while the girl was under fire. So, I charged the building, heading toward a different window on the corner of it. If the sheriff saw me, I was a dead man. No question.

"Think you can come around here and fuck with the law?"

Another shot from the far window. The blast startled me, and I lost my footing, ate dirt, then crawled with the fury of an armadillo on fire toward the corner of the building.

I crouched under the window. With its glass still intact, it was my guess he hadn't seen me. I stuck my head up, peeked in, waiting for a bullet to put me down. Through the window, I could see the sheriff up against the wall, peeking out another window, his focus toward my right, where Nadine sat behind a tree.

I set the rifle down and pulled the pistol, aimed it. He raised his rifle toward Nadine again.

"Come on out you, you peckerwood!" the sheriff screamed.

I fired, and the window shattered. I shut my eyes and ducked.

"Sonofabitch!" It was a pained shout. I'd hit him.

I could hear a shuffling inside—a limping gait. The noise grew louder, closer to the window, then stopped. When I heard a guttural moan directly above me, I raised up and fired. A wet warmth splashed my face, and the unmistakable sound of a body hitting the floor sang like a chorus of angels.

I looked inside and saw no one else. The camp could have still held more, but with no other shots heard and four men dead, I figured the place was clean, though my main concern was making sure Nadine was okay.

I ran across the courtyard and through the cloud of smoke rising from the burning deputy, the smell of charred flesh stinging my nose. When I got to Nadine, she had her legs tucked to her chest, rifle in her tiny arms, making sure no part of her stuck out from the tree she hid behind.

"You okay?" I asked her.

She nodded. "I hit him." It wasn't a prideful declaration, just an acknowledgment that she'd done her part. She'd killed a man.

The line between celebration and mourning the loss of innocence was thin, so the best I could do was offer encouragement. I didn't want the poor girl lying awake nights with the guilt of bloody hands. So, I looked straight into her eyes. "Because of you, we may have saved Franklin. Now, I'm gonna look for him. You stay here and keep a watchful eye."

She said she would, then told me to be careful. I ran a hand through her choppy white hair and kissed her head, then went for the shack. The structure had no windows and was about half the size of the rooms at a cheap inn—the kind meant for an hour of bad sex or sleeping off a hangover. I figured they most likely used it as a holding cell for those they meant to kill, or as housing for those they meant to enslave.

Once I got to the shack, I hid behind it and peeked around both sides, looking for another gunman. I saw nothing, heard nothing, so ran around the front and pulled the plank that lay across the door. When I opened the door, dank air hit me with an oppressively thick cloud of sweat and piss that knocked me back and made me gasp, like I should have chewed the air before taking it in.

"I told you, Jackson. This here's my friend, Garrett." I heard Franklin's voice before I saw him. The shack was dark and so was Franklin.

I waved at the air like it was a curtain needing to be pushed aside, then stepped in the shack. Franklin sat on the dirt floor with his hands together out in front of him and a rope around his neck. The other end of the rope was fed through an eyehook, and his hands were tied to another black man's hands in front of him. I assumed that fella's name was Jackson. He wore a sheet of sweat and the biggest smile I'd ever seen.

"How many you take down?" Franklin asked me.

"Four."

"There's at least five, Garrett."

I froze when he said that. With the doorway facing those dark, brooding windows, all three of us were sitting ducks. When a gunshot broke the ice, everything slowed down. A window shattered, and I felt the wind from a bullet brush the back of my hand, then Jackson's head banged hard against the wall and blood rushed from a newly formed hole near his temple.

Before I had a chance to react, another shot exploded, this time from behind the shack, where Nadine was. I swung my head toward the buildings and saw a man wearing a sheet, standing in the window. He had a clawed hand to his chest, looking like a ghost holding a bright-red flower which bloomed quickly under that hand, then he fell backward and crashed to the floor.

"Damn." Franklin's eyes were on Jackson's lifeless body. Jackson stared back.

I reached up and tugged at the rope. "I don't suppose they let you keep your knife."

"One of them deputies took it."

I looked toward the circle of log benches. "Hold on." I shut the door and ran for the deputy Nadine had shot, praying for silence. If I heard a gunshot here in the open, I'd shit my pants before I was dead. The deputy had no knife, though I did grab the revolver lying next to him.

I ran to the smoldering deputy—black as night, like the charred log on a dying fire. What was left of the knife was stuck to his side. I kicked him, and it fell loose. I grabbed the handle with two fingers like it was a turd I meant to toss, then ran back to the shack with it. I pulled out my handkerchief and wrapped the handle, then cut the rope from Franklin's neck and hands.

"I knew there'd come a day you'd show up. But the same day I'm taken? Wasn't expecting that. Figured I'd be here at least a few months 'fore you worked things out," Franklin said.

"You can thank Nadine for that. She led us straight to you, even picked two of those fuckers off."

"God bless that girl."

We ran to Nadine. She smiled when she saw Franklin, then hugged him. I prayed what she felt in that moment would take the place of any dark thoughts she might have. Thoughts of blood on her hands.

"Thank you, Ms. Nadine." Franklin's eyes were like two orbs of wet glass, and when he squeezed her and shut them, the tears fell.

CHAPTER 11

AFTER SCOUTING THE CAMP, we grabbed bullets, money, and three horses with saddlebags loaded full of food and canteens. I gave Franklin the extra revolver I had, and he took the holster it belonged to and strapped it on.

He asked if we happened to grab his writings from the wagon. We hadn't. "That's alright," he said. "There'll be plenty more stories to tell."

Then there was talk on whether or not we should still hit Branchwood, especially riding the horses we was on. But I speculated that with the lawmen the town was cursed with, we might look like some well-needed heroes. I figured the town was in a state of oppression and depression, and we'd exorcised the demons. Should the locals find that out, perhaps they'd treat us like saviors rather than criminals in need of a hangin'.

It was a dangerous speculation, but Branchwood was the only chance we had of finding Diane's killer. Skipping that next link in the chain could have us wandering in the wrong direction for weeks. Either way, we decided to stay away from the center of town and ask residents on the outskirts. If we was going to happen across trouble, we just as soon not attract a mob and deal with one house at a time.

During the ride, Franklin told us about Jackson. He said the man had been in that shed for weeks. They was using him to stack and chop wood, clean, and start a garden. He also thought they may have been raping him too because he wouldn't ever sit and screamed when shittin'. When he talked about the raping part, he chose words too vague for Nadine to catch.

I told Franklin I was sorry for stirring the pot over at Carlton's, and he said those men would have taken him regardless. "Even if you was handin' out home-baked goods," he said.

I didn't ask him if they made him lick the shit from the dead man's legs.

Rather than stick to the road, we cut through, keeping an eye on where we was headed, making sure Branchwood was still in sight. Houses popped sporadically along the terrain like lone prairie dogs, then the land was peppered with them. From afar, Branchwood seemed to be a busy town. I'd heard of the place but never visited, and seeing how a corrupt bunch wore the badges, I was glad of that.

We kept the town on our right, keeping clear of it, until we started crossing over once the houses became sporadic again.

"If we're gonna head in and start askin' questions, I figure the houses what look like they could use some fixin' would be best. I don't trust anyone here with money. The means of it probably didn't earn them no wings," I said.

Franklin agreed, and Nadine pointed toward a house with a fence that barely stood with every other plank missing like the gapped teeth in an old timer's mouth. There was a piglet roaming around the back door, and when we rode up, Nadine climbed down and gave it some attention.

A woman walked out right then, wiping flour from her hands, and said, "Her name is Pearl. Like pearls of wisdom, cuz she's smart enough not to roll in her own mess." She smiled when she said it, and her eyes had a twinkle to them. She looked to be in her mid-forties, at least ten years older than myself, but gorgeous as the sun after an unwelcome blizzard.

"I'm Nadine." She was crouched, her hands running

along the pig's back. And in that moment, she was a little girl again. Not a young woman. Not an assassin.

"Evening, Nadine. I'm Mary. Pleased to make your acquaintance." The woman tried to curtsy, and her knees popped like beetle carapaces underfoot. She looked at Franklin and me. "Gentlemen."

We both nodded. "Ma'am."

She seemed to be a good choice for interrogation, so I asked her if she'd heard anything about murders in town. I told her outright we was searching for a killer.

I think maybe she was uncomfortable speaking about such things around Nadine, but she answered. "Last murder I heard about was when . . . " She looked at Franklin and hesitated, like he may take offense to what she had to say. " . . . they found a man hanging from a cross in the middle of town. But that was last summer."

"Was a black man, wasn't it?" Nadine stood up.

Mary's eyes darted toward Franklin again, and she offered a timid nod.

"The law find the killer?" Franklin asked. I knew he meant to feel her out about the sheriff's reputation.

She gave a knowing snicker and shook her head. "I think they have an idea. The man you're looking for, who'd he kill?"

"Handful of people, including her mother." I nodded at Nadine who'd gone back to stroking the pig.

The weight of my words sat on the woman's brow and pulled at the corners of her mouth. "I'm so sorry."

"You suppose local law may lend a hand?" Franklin still searching for what we already knew.

"Sir . . . "

"Franklin." He offered a gentle smile that said it was safe to share whatever was on her mind.

"Franklin . . . I'll be honest. If you ride into town asking Sheriff Chancellor for help, on account of your skin, you ain't gettin' it. On the other hand, if your killer is black, there's a chance they done already got him."

"He isn't," Nadine said. "He's a white man, with a crooked mustache, brown hair, and a hole in his back where I stuck him."

Mary looked at us, as though searching for the right words to say, then, "I just ate dinner, and I've got plenty left over. Won't you come in and eat? It's just me here, and if I'm honest I could use the company."

I waited to see what Nadine wanted to do. She hugged the pig, then stood up and brushed her hands off on her dress. "Okay."

Mary looked at me for approval, and I nodded, then climbed off the horse and hitched her to the old fence. Franklin did the same.

While the outside of Mary's house was less than presentable, the inside was clean and quaint, even homey. It smelled of cedar wood, and when she lit a small lantern to fight the oncoming night, the warm glow made me want to lay right there on the floor and go to sleep.

She had a table with four chairs, and I wondered what happened to the family who used to sit at them, if there ever was one. We sat there while she served a hearty stew, then she tended to the dough she was kneading when we showed up.

"Don't suppose you could point us toward the town gossip, or anyone else who keeps their ear to the ground," I said.

"You could might try the Johnston twins. Some say Gabriel Johnston is a seer. Some say he's batshit crazy. All I know is one time he told Jonathan Joseph his cattle would die, and that's just what happened. All in the same night, every one of them butchered. Now, I suppose you could say Gabriel up and did it himself, bein' crazy and all. But some believe something more sinister did it. Some say a man-wolf. Some say Gabriel's a man-wolf his own self."

"A man-wolf?" Nadine asked.

"A man what changes to a wolf by the light of the moon. The moon may pave your way in the night, but it holds secrets and motives we're not privy to, nor should we want to be."

"Holy hell," Nadine whispered, and I gave her a scolding eye.

"Sounds like campfire hogwash," I said, scooping a mouthful of stew.

"Brings to mind the gang over in Spahnson," Franklin said. "They went nuts, thinkin' people was wendigos when they wasn't. Killed all manner of innocent folks."

"That's awful," Mary said.

"They was a cult."

Nadine's eyes trailed out the window, looking for the moon.

"This is damn fine stew, Ms. Mary," Franklin said. He was eating like he hadn't ever been taught how to before. Slurping, shoveling. Wasn't even giving his tastebuds a chance to make a judgment call.

I agreed and thanked the woman for her hospitality. "You know a little about us," I told her. "Wouldn't mind hearing about yourself."

"Not much to say, really. Never had kids, and my husband left me years ago for another woman. I make by here raising hogs . . . " She looked at Nadine and placed a hand on hers. "Don't worry. I'd never slaughter Pearl. I plan to keep her as long as the good Lord allows." Her focus switched back to me. "And I work at the general store a few hours a week. It isn't much, but I ain't starving, and I've got a bed."

Franklin stopped with the shoveling long enough to ask a question. "What are the people like here in Branchwood? I mean . . . is they as kind as you?"

"Most are, yes. There's a few bad apples, the sheriff and his men for starters. But it's quiet overall."

"So, if we head to the inn, they gonna offer me a bed?" Franklin asked.

"I couldn't promise anything. I know Simon. He owns the inn. He's a good man, and he don't like the law around here just as much as the next person, but he's got a business to run and don't like trouble, which means turning blacks away if he thinks the sheriff's got his ear to the door."

"Figured as much. Thank you, Ms. Mary." Franklin dove back into his stew, but with a lot less enthusiasm.

Mary went up behind Franklin and put a hand on his shoulder, rubbed it. "I'm sorry." The way she moved her fingers, all slow and gentle, I couldn't tell if they was driven by sympathy or lust. "I don't have enough room for all of you, but if a couple of you want to sleep in the barn and the other in here, I've got a few extra blankets and would be happy to offer a good night's rest. Least I can do."

Franklin took pause and raised eyes at me. A smile split his face in half. It was clear who'd be sleeping in here and who'd be sleeping in the barn.

"That's awfully thoughtful of you, Mary. But—"

Franklin interrupted right quick. "We appreciate that, thank you. I could certainly use some rest."

It wasn't I was jealous. I was worried. Mary seemed wholesome and genuine. But we didn't know her from Eve, and I was having a rough time trusting strangers anymore. And far as I knew, she was a succubus doing the Klan's work, leading blacks to slaughter. But I didn't want to be the one stopping Franklin from getting some well-needed mud for his turtle, so I agreed to sleep in the barn with Nadine.

After the meal, we helped clean up, then Mary gave Nadine and I a large blanket made up of smaller ones, most likely for saddles. It'd been hand-stitched and seen better days—loose thread and tiny holes.

I thanked Mary and told her to let us know if there's anything we could do before we leave at sunup, then Nadine and I left her and Franklin to fill each other's voids.

There was plenty of room in the barn for the horses, so I brought them in. Nadine and I made makeshift beds in the far corner. We set our rifles nearby, and I kept my revolver even closer.

As we lay there in the dark, the moon casting a beam on us through a gap in the planks, Nadine asked what her mom was like when we was young.

"She was a lot like you. Determined, strong, and beautiful. Smart too."

"She didn't have pink eyes and white hair, though."

"No, she didn't. She missed out on those blessings."

"I don't think they're blessings." I could hear the pain in the statement.

"I can understand that. When you're young, it's hard to appreciate being unique. It feels like you don't fit nowhere. You want to be like everyone else. But when you get older, that fades away."

"But you're not different, so how do you know that's how it is?"

"You must have not looked at my eyes real close before." I sat up, placed myself right in the moonbeam, and opened my eyes wide so she could get a look.

She sat up, scooched toward me, then squinted. "Are they different colors?"

"Sure are. Probably hard to tell in here, but you catch me under the sun tomorrow and you'll see one blue and one green."

"And you didn't like that?"

"Not one bit. Until I got older and embraced it. Also, between you and me, the ladies seem to like it. I've no doubt when you get some years on you, a young man is gonna see your skin and those eyes and think you're the most perfect creature God ever blessed the earth with."

Nadine went quiet after that. I knew the last few words meant nothing to her now. But when her eyes started wandering toward the boys and she felt even more like an outcast, thinking ain't no man ever going to want to make her his bride, I was hoping that's when the words would surface again and do some healing, like a balm on an open wound.

She looked at my eyes once more, then laid back down and stuck her arm up, letting the moonbeam fall across her hand.

"Uncle Garrett? Do you think man-wolves are real?"

"I think God put some mysterious beings on the planet, but I don't think man-wolves are one of them. But if they do exist, they're not nearly as frightening as mankind."

I meant for the words to give her solace, but when I replayed them in my head, I wasn't sure that's how they landed. Nevertheless, she fell asleep before I did. I stayed awake another hour, fighting the tears I'd managed to deny thus far.

CHAPTER 12

WE WOKE AT DAWN. Other than a few uncomfortable moments when the hay decided to test its strength against my ribs, I slept through the night with no troubles. Nadine said she had too, except for the nightmares. She said they was filled with man-wolves and other stuff, which I took to mean losing her momma and being raped. That's a lifetime of nightmare fuel.

We folded the blankets and headed to the house. I knocked on the back door in case Franklin and Mary weren't decent, or going another round.

Nobody answered.

I knocked again. Still nothing.

I knocked a third time, and the old door rattled like it might come off if I go any harder. When nobody came or called out, I went to a window and put my hands up to it, peeked in.

Franklin was lying on the floor face down, and Mary was spread out across the bed.

Just like Diane.

My throat tightened and my heart punched my ribs. I ran to Nadine. "You listen here. I need you to close your eyes and keep 'em closed. Hold onto my belt and don't let go."

"He get Mary and Franklin?"

I crouched down and looked at her—a porcelain doll cracked by a frown and a furrowed brow. "Don't look."

"Did he?" She started wiping tears that hadn't even come yet.

"Dammit, girl. Don't you look. You hear me?"

She nodded, then covered her eyes, and grabbed my belt with her free hand.

I opened the door, gun drawn, scanned the room. It was empty. The bedroom door was open. I walked Nadine over to the table, sat her in a chair, and faced it toward the wall.

"Stay here," I told her. She slapped a hand to her mouth, started whimpering.

From where I stood, I could see Franklin's bare legs. And Mary's glistening entrails—wet snakes frozen mid slither.

With each step toward the door, the old floor made the announcement I was coming. If the killer was in the bedroom, he heard every step, and now this was nothing more than a game we were playing, each of us waiting on the other's move. Finally, I figured whether I was creeping in or charging didn't much matter. One of us was gonna go down, and it wasn't going to be me, so I rushed into the room, spinning to my left, and kicking the door wide in case he was behind it. Except for the visceral aftermath, the room was empty. He'd killed and left without me hearing so much as a rusty hinge in the wee hours.

I looked down at Franklin and saw the skin intact—back, ass, and legs clear of injury and blood. But as I crouched to flip him over, I prepared for a faceless mask I'd never forget. I turned to the doorway, made sure Nadine hadn't snuck behind with rebellious curiosity, then grabbed Franklin's shoulder and pulled, flipping him over.

His face was there. Everything was there, but his lips were covered in congealed blood that seemed to come from his nose. Then I saw his ribs expand, and he moaned. Thank you, Jesus, Franklin was alive.

"Franklin." I shook him a little. He opened his eyes, blinked a dozen or so times. I could see everything coming back to him, then he swung his head toward the bed, saw Mary, sighed, and dropped his head to the floor where it bounced with a painful knock. "Thank God you're in one piece. The hell happened?"

"That fucker was here last night . . . or this morning. I can't be sure. It was still dark though." Franklin grabbed the top of his head and pulled at his hair, then his eyes went wide, and he shot up like a rattler striking out. "Where's Nadine!?"

"She's in the other room. She's safe."

I saw Franklin look at something behind me, and I knew it was my niece. I turned. "Dammit, Nadine." I slumped on the floor with my back to the wall, exhausted from the rush of fear. "How the hell am I supposed to keep you outta harm's way when you're pickin' and choosin' when and when not to listen?"

She ignored me. "You okay, Franklin?" Her tiny little voice didn't belong in that bloody room. It was like a lily in a drought.

He realized he was still naked and covered his junk quick-like with his hands. "My noggin' hurts is all."

"Did you see him? Did you see his crooked mustache?"

"All I seen was a shadow. I remember hearing the window open, then footsteps. By the time I was outta bed to check, he was in the doorway. That's all I remember. Now, if you'll excuse me, Ms. Nadine, I need to make myself decent."

"Sorry." Nadine followed the trail of Mary's intestines with her eyes, then walked away.

Franklin stood slowly, grabbing his head. "Worse than a hangover."

"We'll get you some water and something in your belly."

"Not here we won't," Franklin wrestled with his pants, which had somehow missed getting bloody despite lying on the floor. "We need to get the hell outta here. Don't matter I didn't cut this woman up. They see a black man slept in this house and now a woman's dead, they'll have a noose around my neck faster than a bird shits."

While Franklin seemed to avoid eyeing Mary, I got a better look. More than I should have. Other than her belly split and her insides on the outside, her nipples were missing just like the others, and I think her vagina was too. It was such a mess down there I couldn't be sure. Either way, he'd done a number on her.

But what really bothered me was Nadine had seen it. That girl had seen more than most men and women do in a couple lifetimes. I couldn't be sure how she viewed the world anymore, but I can't imagine she held much hope for anything or anyone, except maybe killing the man what took that hope.

"Something that don't make sense about this is I ain't dead, "Franklin said. "Why didn't he skin me like he did the other men?"

"It's a good question. I can think of maybe two reasons. One being that if he don't kill any blacks then it's the blacks they'll go looking for. A scapegoat. The other being that he don't like dark meat. And if that's the case, I suppose this could be the one time you being black has paid off."

Franklin rubbed his head. "Ain't that something."

Continuing to keep his eyes from Mary, Franklin kissed his fingertips and touched the bed. "You was a good woman, Mary. A damn fine woman." Then he grabbed his shirt and boots and gun, and we hustled out to the barn with Nadine.

We searched for tracks, and that was useless. The ground was dry, and none of us were much good at tracking anyhow. We may as well been trying to build a steam engine using twigs and bark.

"I'd like to know if he hit any other house around here, but I ain't about to go door to door and find out." Franklin climbed on his horse. "Another thought I had is him following us, and this is some game he's playin'."

"Bullshit. He ain't following us. He's got no idea we're on his tail. Was a coincidence is all." The only thing that was bullshit were my own words. The killer following us was exactly what I was thinking. But I couldn't let Nadine think she wasn't safe, always having to look over her shoulder.

"When we was in bed last night, Mary mentioned them twins again. The Johnston brothers," Franklin said. "She seemed to be convinced maybe they could help. Could be worth payin' them a visit."

"The crazy man who may or may not be a seer?"

"The man-wolf?" Nadine said.

"Ain't no man-wolves about, Nadine. We talked about this," I told her.

Franklin grabbed the reins. "I know you think it's hogwash, Garrett. But unless you got a better idea—"

"It is hogwash. Fortune-telling . . . magic . . . voodoo . . . "

"You leave voodoo out of it. I don't know much about readin' palms and stars or tellin' futures, but I know voodoo. Seen too much of it not to believe."

I sighed and looked over at Nadine. Her wide eyes showed excitement at the prospect of the fantastic. "Alright, friend. She happen to tell you where they can be found?"

"Matter of fact, she did."

CHAPTER 13

WE WEREN'T ABOUT to show our faces in the middle of Branchwood. Just like Franklin had said, we were sure to be linked to Mary's death once they found her. Strangers passing through town, and one of them a black man? There'd be no investigation, only accusation. Fortunately, the directions Mary had given were to follow a dried creek bed away from town. We was to follow that until we seen an old red post near a copse of trees. The post marked an overgrown path that went through the woods and straight to the Johnston house. The directions Mary gave were more than adequate, and we found the trail with no problem.

The trail was narrow, so we rode single file—me upfront and Franklin taking the rear. I turned behind me and watched Nadine's face for a grimace, making sure the ride was treating her okay. It seemed the night's rest had helped, because her face was free of pain, her eyes catching the forest scenery.

About a half hour passed before we saw the house up ahead. I stopped and made sure everyone understood I should do the talking until we felt them out, then I handed Nadine my pistol and told her to hide it in her dress if she could. She drove the gun down her front and tucked it somewhere along her waist. It may have been a bad idea. I didn't know how quick she could get to it or how uncomfortable it may be. But if something happened where I wasn't right there, I'd like to know she had it.

The house was like nothing I ever seen before. Two giant boxes joined by a sort of wooden tunnel. One side was covered in stained glass windows like a church. No pictures were depicted, just a collage of broken colors. On top of it was a steeple made from old wood, towering at least 12 feet above the roof.

The other side of the house was covered in pinecones, like they'd been nailed up one by one. The windows were amber in color, like the glow from a fireplace at night, except it was early morning.

Each section had a door, as did the tunnel between. The church-style building's door said "Gabriel," and the pinecone door said "Alexander." The middle door read "Johnston."

I looked at Franklin. "Nope. This ain't hogwash. This is batshit crazy, just like Mary said."

"Maybe . . . but we're here, so we may as well find out for sure."

"I think it's pretty," Nadine said.

"Pretty for a dollhouse, not so much a grown man's house," I said.

We rode up quietly, nonthreatening like, and parked the horses.

"Well, pick a door, Garrett." Franklin thought this was funny and chuckled.

I walked up to the door in the middle that said Johnston and knocked. A few moments later, there was a scuffling inside the wooden structure like two giant kittens wrestling. When the door opened, there were two men standing there, paws on each other, holding one another back, like being the first to the door was some kind of contest. Both men were shorter than myself, heavyset and sweaty, like two overgrown babies with full heads of hair. Identical twin babies, except one wore only his undergarments and was barefoot. That man had on a necklace with a turquoise stone that dangled down to his belly. The other man wore regular work attire, which was stained and scuffed from hard labor, or maybe just from wrestling in that hallway when visitors showed. It was easy to tell which one was Gabriel the Seer.

"Afternoon, gentlemen," I said.

The man in the undergarments and dangling turquoise pushed his way out of the door first. "Visitors!" His arms opened wide like he was displaying himself, or wanting a hug. His brother stood in the threshold, arms across his chest and resting on his belly.

"My name's Garrett Walkinshaw. This here's my best friend in all the world, Franklin."

Turquoise man smiled, and his teeth were the straightest I'd ever seen. Big like a horse's and white as ivory. "This is my brother Alexander. And I'm his brother, Gabriel."

"Howdy," Alexander said. His teeth were big too and just as straight, but not as white.

After a few rounds of howdys and hellos, I said, "We come here under some fairly unique circumstances, and was wondering if you—"

"You need my help," Gabriel said matter-of-factly.

"I take it you get the request often."

"Nope. I just know a needin' face when I see one."

I caught Alexander rolling his eyes. They may have been twins, but they weren't on the same page.

"Well, you're right about that. We do need some help, whether it's you that can offer it, we'll see. Anyhow, we was sent by . . . " I looked at Franklin who gave a subtle shake of his head. " . . . someone, and they said you might be able to help track . . . a killer." Once the words left my mouth, it took all I had to keep my head up. Asking for help from a half-naked man who lived in a church playhouse for kids made as much sense as asking a dog for tips on how to wipe my own ass.

"Of course, of course," Gabriel said, with a little too much excitement. I glanced at his brother who looked about as lively as a turtle drunk on molasses. "Come on in. We'll head into the chapel. You can tell me all about it."

We headed through the Johnston door and followed Gabriel as he led us down the tunnel—which resembled a hallway from the inside. Alexander stood at the door, letting us in. Once the Johnston door was shut, the hallway was dimly lit by a hundred different colors from the light pouring in through the stained glass ahead.

"I'm so glad you decided to come here for help. Not many people make it out this way, and I rarely get a chance to show off the chapel." Gabriel walked through the chapel door and stepped to the side, then held his arm out wide, leading us in and presenting his pride and joy.

There wasn't much to the room, except the walls, which were covered in stained glass, though they looked better in here than they did outside, the sun casting colorful shapes about the floor and on what little bit of wall there was. Toward the back of the room was some sort of pulpit made from a pig's trough tipped on its side, which had a cross nailed to the front of it.

For a minute, I thought Gabriel meant for us to stand around while he gave a sermon behind the trough, but then he sat on the ground—which looked as though it got a regular sweeping—patted it and asked us to join him. We did, though his brother stood by the doorway, arms still folded.

"Tell me about your needs," Gabriel said, a childish grin across his horse-teeth mouth.

Franklin spoke up. "Well, we been travelin' since yesterday morning, following a brown-haired man with a scar across his lip, and it seems we've come to a standstill. Not sure which way to head now."

I looked over at Alexander and got the impression he didn't hold much faith in his brother so I shouldn't either, which I didn't.

I said, "His last murder was over in Branchwood. I'm not sure what you can do with so little infor—"

Gabriel burst out in some kind of howl, his eyes closed and face toward the ceiling. Previous talk of man-wolves crossed my mind, and I glanced at Nadine, whose eyes were bigger than I'd ever seen and lit brighter than usual by the stained glass.

The man stopped howling but kept his eyes closed. He reached his hands out, shook them impatiently, and said, "Join hands."

I grabbed his hand and Franklin grabbed the other. Nadine just sat there between us, frozen.

"The circle's broken. Someone hasn't joined hands," Gabriel said, then opened his eyes. "Girl . . . you need to—" His eyes went wide, and he pulled his hand from mine like it was a viper meant to strike. "What abomination have you brought into my chapel?"

"Gabriel!" Alexander said behind us. "They need your help. That's all."

With a trembling hand, Gabriel pointed at Nadine. "She's got the devil's eyes."

"Whoa. You hold on just a minute," I said.

"Demons running free in her!"

I stood up. So did Franklin. Nadine sat, spooked by the accusation, as well as the howl.

Alexander approached his brother. "Gabe! Calm the fuck down! Ain't no demon in that girl."

"I can see it clear as day. The taint of spilled blood swimming in them orbs. Bone-white flesh. It all makes sense now. You didn't come for help. You came to unleash all of hell in my chapel."

Franklin and I both threw hands toward our guns, ready to blow the nut's head clean off. Before I had a chance to consider further, Alexander drew his gun fast as lightning. But he didn't aim at me, Franklin, or Nadine. He aimed at the biggest window in the room—an impressive piece of glass that looked like a field of misshapen flowers under a melting sun.

"I swear I'll bust right through that glass, Gabriel Johnston. Then what you gonna do? Every demon you've ever kept at bay will come rushing through here."

"You wouldn't dare!"

"Leave the girl alone and get to the house. You've done all you can, and it ain't been for shit. It's time you realize that."

"Now, why in God's name would I let a demon leave the sanctuary when I got it trapped right here?"

"She ain't no demon, Gabe. She's just different is all." He looked down at Nadine and offered a gentle smile. "Now get to the house and put yourself to bed or I'm putting a bullet straight through the window, and I won't stop until the gun's empty."

Like a child being punished, Gabriel lowered his head and ran toward the hall, down it, then slammed a door on the other end.

Alexander holstered his pistol, leaned down, and took Nadine's hand, helped her off the floor. He looked at Franklin and myself. "My apologies. I been sitting idly by, letting my brother do his thing, only cuz I know it makes him happy. This here is normally a harmless ordeal. A few hand-holdin' prayers, some oddball declarations, and gibberish he thinks is tongue speakin'. He means well, but as you can see, he ain't right in the head."

Alexander went on to tell us about how years ago his brother developed a curiosity for Indian culture.

"It was an obsession, really. He studied what he could, watched from afar, and even had a few conversations with some locals that'd left their tribes. The bits Gabriel couldn't put together in his studies, he guessed on, and that led to his experimenting with mescaline. Once he tried it, that was the end of the Gabriel I used to know. What came out on the other side of his vision quest, as he called it, was a demented and broken man scared of his own shadow, blaming demons for everything from harsh weather to a bad fart.

"If you really want help the likes of which Gabe pretends to know, I'd seek out Lady Bethlehem. Her means are . . . unconventional, but accurate. She ain't crazy like my brother is, though she will test your fear of the unknown. But as far as getting my brother's help, you're just chasing your tail here. He ain't no seer, just likes to think so. Again, my apologies. Especially to you, little lady."

I looked at Franklin. "See? Batshit hogwash."

Nadine gave me a nasty side eye, then turned to Alexander. "What if you're wrong? What if he just seems crazy cuz he's holding so much truth?"

Alexander's kind smile was offered again. "Well . . . you see this stained glass here? According to Gabriel, it's to keep the demons out, specifically during the day when the sun cleanses the house with its angelic reflections. And those pinecones covering the house . . . that's to trap lost souls. When a pinecone falls from it, my brother takes it as a sign a soul has hit the house and trapped itself within the seed. From there, he buries it in the woods to give the soul a chance to reach Heaven once the tree grows tall enough. Now, you gonna trust that kinda logic? 'Cuz I sure as hell ain't."

Nadine's head fell in disappointment. "Well . . . what makes Lady Bethlehem any different? I bet some call her crazy too."

"That they do, but only those who ain't ever met her. If you go there, you'll see the difference between nuts and legitimacy."

I had to admit, I was intrigued. Even if I didn't believe in any of it. "Alright, where can we find her?"

"Ever been to Sleepybrook?"

"Ain't even heard of it," I said. Franklin said he hadn't either.

"It ain't nothing but a piss stain on the map that I wouldn't call a town as much I would a cemetery. Only people what live there are dead ones, and ones on their way to bein' dead. Old folks. Real old." He waved us toward the door and walked down the hall. "Once you hit the main road, keep heading west until you hit Hangman's Canyon. You'll know it when you see it." He opened the Johnston door, and we all headed outside. I could hear Gabriel in the house, cussing and bitchin' about being sent away. "Once you pass through the canyon, you'll hit a fork. Head south. It ain't much of a road but enough to follow until you hit a dead forest, burned up years ago and ain't ever grown back. Just beyond that is Sleepybrook. You'll have to ask from there. They'll know how to find her."

I thanked him for everything, especially for taming his brother.

"He won't be tame for long, so if I were you, I'd hit the road."

"Is it 'cuz he's a man-wolf?" Nadine asked.

"Nadine!" I said.

The man tried to offer another one of those gentle smiles, but it shriveled and died like a leech under salt. "Best get goin'." Then he turned and disappeared behind the pinecone door.

As we rode away, I could hear the muffled sound of Gabriel's howl.

CHAPTER 14

WE MADE A few stops before nightfall to stretch our legs, eat, and give the horses a rest. By our third stop, we'd reached what was undoubtedly Hangman's Canyon. It was a rocky patch of land sunk down in the earth. The ground was bare, save for a few trees that poked up from the ground, all sporting thick branches that stuck out like arms meant to hold a lengthy noose, like gallows made by God. We found an alcove off the road that made for decent shelter against the wind that'd picked up and decided to camp there for the night.

Franklin rode out and gathered broken limbs, while I collected dead brush for a fire. By the time all was done, there was enough for a fire that'd burn hot but quick, enough to heat some beans, and our toes should the night change its mind on the weather.

While riding the horses made for faster travel, I missed the convenience of the wagon, able to carry whatever load we'd need, rather than just the bare essentials. Not to mention Nadine was back to limping again. Not as much as the day before, but bad enough to take notice. I made her rest while we tended to the fire and made dinner. After she fell asleep, Franklin and I got to talking.

"What makes a man strip a person of their parts like they was prey? Like they was nothin' but hide and a meal?" Franklin said.

"Don't rightly know. But it's a question I hope to ask the man personally. Right before I set his eyes apart."

"Appreciate you giving Gabriel a shot, and now this Lady Bethlehem," Franklin said. "I know you ain't partial to unconventional means of doin' things."

"Don't have much of a choice. We're in a bind, ain't we? Couldn't go to town, couldn't ask the law . . . what might be left of them."

"Might coulda if you didn't have a black man at your side."

I stared Franklin down. "You listen here. You're the best man I know . . . best man I'll ever know. You ain't no albatross around my neck."

"Shit . . . that ain't the way I see it. I nearly got you and Nadine killed back at the Klan's base."

"No . . . I nearly got us killed, for recognizing your worth and goin' after it. Ain't your fault the world's got fuckers like them, thinkin' they can use a man like he's an animal."

"Well, I'm grateful, just so you know. But do me a favor . . . that happens again, leave me to rot. I'd rather die than know one of you got harmed on account of me."

"Let's just make sure it never happens again, friend."

By the light of the fire, I could see Franklin's eyes well up with tears. He brushed them away before they fell. "So . . . what happens if this Lady Bethlehem can't help? We headin' back home?"

I hadn't given it much thought. Hadn't allowed myself to think there was any other outcome than seeing the killer bleeding out. But if we found ourselves at a dead end, I couldn't drag my niece around the world with the hopes we'd find more bodies stripped of skin just to start the trail afresh. I told Franklin that.

"Yeah, I get it," he said. "That ain't no life for a child."

"It's a tough call. If we don't find him, none of us are satisfied, and I don't know how rested her nights will be. Lying awake, wondering if the man will find her. Then again, wanderin' on the road ain't much of a life for anyone."

"Nadine's strong. She don't think like most girls, I reckon. Maybe ask her what she wants to do when the time comes."

"Yeah, maybe," I said. "I just worry about what she's seen . . . what she's done. It's changing her."

"It's how the skin sheds, Garrett. None of us stay young. Mind or body. The world has a way of bringin' on the molt, sometimes tearing it off before you're ready."

And with that, we let the night pull us in deep, resting in its quiet arms, while I dreamt of skinned bodies and man-wolves, hoping Franklin dreamt of a freedom he deserved and would always have.

CHAPTER 15

WE WOKE UP just before dawn. All together. All skin intact. We ate sparingly, leaving some for lunch and dinner. I asked Nadine if she had nightmares again and she had, though didn't share them. I wondered if we found the madman the nightmares might stop.

As we were saddling the horses, I recalled Franklin talking in his sleep the night before. He'd been going on about Mary, apologizing. It was my guess he carried the weight of her death, though if one of us is to blame—that is if he'd been following us and playing games—it was me. I'm the one who started the hunt and dragged my friend into it.

"Mary wasn't your fault, you know," I said to him.

He looked at me like I had two heads, and his eyes turned to glass like he might cry again. Then he turned away and fed his horse an apple. Moments later, I heard him sniffle, saw him run a sleeve across his face.

I couldn't be sure what time it was, but we were on the road well before noon, the three of us forming a wall of dust in the road, eyes on the lookout for a dead forest. A few hours went by, and we saw our first person since leaving Branchwood. The three of us slowed, got a good look at him, checking for a harelip as he passed by. I nodded, and he kept his eyes ahead like we weren't even there—three ghosts who didn't know they was dead.

After he passed, I shouted, "You happen to know if we're close to the dead forest?"

He said nothing, just rode on.

Franklin pointed out buzzards circling above. A small part of me hoped it was because somewhere up ahead lay a woman with her nipples gone, maybe a man missing his flesh. Anything at all that told us we were still on track and need not be so desperate as to seek out some witch in the woods.

We kept one eye on the birds and the other on the road. Eventually, the birds landed, and we went off the trail just enough to see their meal was nothing more than a rabbit. The way the birds fought over the furry carcass reminded me we're not that different. Mankind is evil. All for selfish gain is what it boils down to. Whether that be money, fame, property, or a perverted fetish. Pleasures of the flesh one way or another.

When we rode away from the snapping buzzards, I wondered about my own selfish gain—revenge—and knew I didn't much give a shit how it looked, just so long as the man stopped breathing.

CHAPTER 16

THE HORIZON WAS BLACK, like a caterpillar laid across the plains, its furry back poking up from the ground. It was the dead forest up ahead, and before long, we was riding through it.

Trees stabbed the sky like giant charred ribs, and the air was thick with the reek of musty charcoal. Not a single leaf nor blade of grass lived among the vast black canvas. A few birds steadied themselves on the roots of weak limbs that jutted from the blackened trunks, but no song escaped them. Even the sky seemed to change color from bright blue to a brown-gray the deeper we found ourselves, as though the trees themselves polluted the air with their reminder of the fire and their aversion to growth and new life.

I'd expected the forest to be smaller than it was, just a patch of trees maybe, like a landmark you could miss if you veered too far left or right. But it was immense, like a black sea of stalagmites, littered with the bones of creatures that once called the place home.

"I don't like it here," Nadine said.

I didn't either. Despite the openness, it was downright suffocating, with every twenty feet or so being met with the stark pale-white of bone peeking through stretched hide.

We picked up the pace to a near gallop, riding with a gap between us so as not to eat the black dust of the other. Nadine's face was covered in worry, and for the next hour she was a little girl again, scared and unsure, and I was the strong uncle meant to protect her.

When the black spikes gave way to a golden meadow, the oppressive cloud lifted, and the sky exploded blue. Once we were in the grasp of the clean air, we stopped and drank.

"So, I'm guessin' Sleepybrook is somewhere up ahead," Franklin said.

I knew he was apprehensive about hitting town. Walking the same streets as a white man without a slave's attire was still fresh, and a roll of the dice on whether or not you were gonna get shit for it. I often told him that with each passing year we'd find less heads up asses. I wasn't sure I believed the words myself, but it was a hope of mine.

"According to the crazy man's brother," I said.

"Maybe we could stay at an inn tonight," Nadine said.

"Still a lot of day ahead of us yet and with no clear notion on where we'll be. But I think that's a fine idea should we find ourselves here come nightfall."

"Wouldn't mind some time to write a little. These past few days got me a headful of words I'd just as soon leave on paper. Maybe something you oughta try too, Nadine. Helps keep the demons out."

"Demons?" Her eyes went wide and her face slack.

"Not demons, demons. Bad thoughts, nightmares. Stuff you'd rather wasn't there. We seen a lot, you and I, and ain't none of what we seen good for anybody. Using a pen gets that out, gives it something to do."

I made a mental note to find Franklin some paper in town. He hadn't picked up a pen since we hit the road, and that wasn't like him. Most days, he'd have a pen in hand more than a drunk held a bottle.

Late one night, while we was at his shithole shack, perched around a fire, he read one of his stories aloud. I could tell it wasn't no make believe but something he'd been through—about a boy who lived at the plantation. The boy snuck food to the others, was eventually caught and punished by removing his winter clothes. He died a few days later. Froze to death in the middle of the night. By the time Franklin reached the end of the story, I had to wipe my eyes dry. I ain't ever read a book before, so I don't know if the writing held up against the ones they publish in them sensation books, but it sure did a number on me. I thought about that heartbreaking tale for weeks, and every cold night since, when I'm throwing on an extra blanket to keep warm.

"Then we need to get you both some proper paper," I said.

Franklin's face lit up, then he looked off, and I could tell he was already choosing the first few words he'd dirty the paper with the first chance he got, letting them demons go.

After a quick bite to eat, we headed out. Within the hour, we spotted our first Sleepybrook building in the distance. And it was on fire.

CHAPTER 17

WE RACED TOWARD the fire. Two horses and a few pigs ran from the blazing structure. They were ablaze too, and all fled in separate directions like giant embers popping from a campfire. The sounds they made was more nightmare fuel.

Nadine started yelling about how we needed to do something, but there was nothing we could do. Eventually, each creature dropped, one at a time, and the little fires went out, as though the flames knew their job was done.

A man and a woman stood in the road watching the engulfed building, which looked to be a barn. The scenario seemed to be the best case if you're going to have a raging fire like this. Could have been their house. Could have been people running through the street all lit up and screaming.

"Sorry about your animals," Franklin got off his horse and stood next to the man who had leathery skin much like the deputy Nadine had killed, except this man's skin sagged from age, with a face like tree bark. He kept rubbing the wisp of hair on top of his head like there were answers up there as to how he'd possibly get on without his pigs and horses.

The man paid no mind to us, and just watched his barn burn, standing in a heat that was darn near unbearable with the sun's two cents.

Nadine hopped down and stood next to the woman—whose face looked carved from the same tree as the man—and took the woman's hand in hers.

I felt like the rude boy at a vigil, so I hopped down too and stood silently like I was paying my respects, waiting for someone to say kind words about the barn and what lived in it.

There was no part of barn wood that wasn't being licked by flame, just a giant, orange block that cracked and popped, moments from crashing to the ground. The air was filled with the smell of bacon, and whatever the hell cooked horse smells like. Smoke rose from their dying spots peppered around the property and down the path toward town.

"That witch bitch did this." The man's voice was like gravel under hoof, an airy, raw-throat grit from years of too much whiskey. I had a feeling Lady Bethlehem's name was about to come up.

"Dammit, Henry," the woman said. "I done told you the horse kicked the kid and sent the lantern flyin'. I seen it. Lady Bethlehem had nothin' to do with this."

And there it was. Barely into Sleepybrook, and we found ourselves a couple that could help steer us. It was a sick kind of irony their house being a torched beacon that would lead us forward.

"Well . . . then she got in that horse's head, made it kick that poor boy."

"Where's the boy?" Nadine said.

They both pointed toward the flames, and suddenly I wondered if the pleasant smell of bacon wasn't bacon after all, and that's when my moment of silence was no longer for the couple's lost property but for the poor boy inside, which they didn't seem too broken up about.

"Where can we find this Lady Bethlehem?" I asked.

Finally, the man broke his gaze and looked at me. His face was so filled with grief it seemed to be melting. "You gonna get revenge?" The word revenge lifted his face into something that resembled a smile.

Then the woman swung her head around. "Don't you dare! That woman ain't done nothin', dammit!"

"We was hopin' she could help us," Franklin said.

A dozen folds appeared in the man's brow. "Help? From a witch?"

"She ain't no damn witch!" The woman slapped the man on the forehead. He didn't even flinch. She looked at Franklin and smiled. Her face cracked like an eggshell, and her too-wet eyes twinkled. "She's over in the marsh, other side of town. Got all manner of strange stones and totems 'round the house. Can't miss it."

I thanked the woman and told them both I was real sorry about their losses. Franklin and I got back on our horses. Nadine said a few kind words to the woman I couldn't quite hear, then offered her a hug.

"You're signing a pact with the devil," the man said, then the woman smacked him again. I held back a chuckle and looked at Franklin. If he was a lighter shade of black, I'd be able to see the red in his face as he held back too.

Nadine hopped on, and we rode past the smoldering beasts. I looked down at one of the horses that lay in the middle of the road, crumpled much the same way Bones was. My heart sunk a little, then a smile came out of nowhere when I recalled the lawmen that killed him and how it turned out for them. I patted my new horse—a handsome brown fella spattered white like he'd caught a splash of milk—then whispered the word "Vengeance" just loud enough for him to hear, as that was his name now.

CHAPTER 18

AS WE RODE through the middle of Sleepybrook, I saw the outskirts were filled with tombstones of varying sizes like the town was centered in the middle of an enormous graveyard.

We met eyes with several locals, and there was nothing but smiles, waves, and verbal greetings from the onlookers, some of which I questioned whether they could even see too far past their own outstretched hands, as every one of them were elderly, and quite a few with cloudy eyes. But the biggest shocker wasn't the friendly hospitality—especially toward Franklin—or the fact that every citizen looked to be older than Adam, with enough wrinkles to store water for a drought, but the black man wearing a badge.

As we made our way toward a general store that'd been nothing more than propped between two other buildings like it just may fall should you sneeze too hard, the lawman walked out and greeted us in the middle of the road. He had a real proud gait but not cocky, not arrogant. Just enough swagger to let us know who's boss, gently so. His mustache covered most of his lip, keeping him younger than he probably was, and his graying hair poofed out under his hat like he'd stuffed a sleeping cat under there.

"Welcome to Sleepybrook. Just passin' through, I presume?"

By the look of everyone we'd seen so far, and remembering what Alexander had told us, I got the feeling if you were gonna be in Sleepybrook for more than a visit you'd need a foot in the grave or on your deathbed. This village was home for the elderly only, like some sort of purgatory—the last stop for those with creaking backs and popping knees, pruned skin and cataract eyes.

"Yessir, just passin' through. And I gotta say, you've got yourself a nice town here. Real kind folks."

The lawman squinted as he looked up at me, and I couldn't tell if he was smiling or keeping the sun out of his aging eyes. Then he put his hand over his brow and shade fell across his face, and the squint went away.

He looked at Franklin and smiled for real this time. "Glad to see you safe, brother."

"You too, although it looks like trouble never found you . . . what I mean is . . . looks like you've made a name for yourself."

I knew what Franklin meant to say, and it was most definitely not out of spite or envy. He had no competitive bones in him when it come to other black folks and who met a harder road than who. I knew he was genuinely happy for the man, whether he was born with a silver spoon or a back full of scars.

"No, you're right, young man. I'm probably the only negro you'll ever meet that hasn't shed a tear over dog scraps or taken a beating. And there ain't a day goes by I'm not grateful for it."

"I'm Franklin." Franklin bent way down and took the old man's hand in his. They shook firmly, proudly. "This here's Garrett, and his niece Nadine."

He nodded. "Garrett . . . Ms. Nadine. I'm Sheriff Garner Shelton. Been the sheriff here for ten years now." He stuck a finger in the gray cloud on his head and scratched. "What brings you through Sleepybrook?"

Considering the other man's opinion of Lady Bethlehem, I was hesitant to bring it up, but Franklin sang immediately. I think he probably felt so comfortable around a black sheriff he would have told him where gold was buried on our way to get it. Only thing he left out was why we was looking for her.

"You won't find too many men 'round here who are fond of her, I'll tell ya that. Some say wives would visit and come back a whole different woman. Less submissive, even downright cruel, degradin' their husbands. Only sign I ever seen of that was when the man deserved it, spending all his money on whores and liquor and the woman got tired of it. Got enlightened. But these men start hollerin' about witchcraft and the devil. I don't get involved in domestics like that unless they turn violent. And only time I caught sight of that was with Mr. McCloud and his wife Annabelle. He took to swingin' at her, but the man was so old he couldn't knock a petal off a dead daisy. Speakin' of which, he started pushin' daises not two days later. Some of these men called that witchcraft too. Said it was Lady Bethlehem's doing. A lesson to all men not to hit their wives. Some of these suspicious folk didn't even think to consider the man was 94 years old. At that age, you're already countin' worms. Only a matter of days. Minutes maybe."

Franklin laughed. He sure did like the sheriff. So did I. A real ray of sunshine.

"How come everyone here's old?" Nadine said.

I went to correct her, but the sheriff seemed to find humor in her loose tongue and more than happy to answer the blatant question.

"You ain't the first one to ask, darlin'. What it boils down to is feeling safe. Age don't welcome a speedy life, and things is slow around here. We ain't got no bank to rob and no saloon to wrangle drunken anger. We got a whorehouse, sure. But that's run by the ladies, and . . . " He stopped himself, realizing his audience was maybe too young to hear about such things. " . . . It's about feeling safe. When you're old like us, time does funny things, and not just to your body but to your mind. You ain't what you used to be, don't like what you used to like. When you take all these like-minded and put them together, it just works. And so that's why everyone here ain't below 65 years of age, which keepin' that rule falls on me. That's my job as sheriff, to make sure a visit is a visit."

"I take it you don't have an inn then," I said.

"No sir, we do not. Our arms are open to any and all throughout the day, and you'll come to meet some of the friendliest people this side of Jesus, but come nightfall you best be gone."

An old man walked out of the general store moving about as fast as sap on a cold day. He smiled at us with a thick black line where teeth once lived. "Howdy, Garner . . . Howdy, folks. Just passin' through?"

"Yes, Hobbs. Just passin' through." The sheriff said it with a reassuring but annoyed tone, as though this were a continual concern each time a new face showed up.

"You have yourselves a good day then," Hobbs said.

"Well, folks. I suppose I ought to get to making my rounds. You need anything at all, I'm easy to find." He turned to leave, then swung back around fairly quick for a man his age. "Oh . . . just a friendly reminder . . . this is a daylight visit only." He patted the gun at his side like it was nothing more than a kind gesture, then winked and walked away.

"Was that a threat?" I whispered to Franklin.

"If it was, I got no problem heedin' it. I like these people. Strange people. But I like what they're doing. Taking life easy. Keepin' trouble at bay, even if it means gettin' ugly."

We rode through the center of the small town, smiles and waves from all directions, almost to the point of making me uncomfortable, like we was the special guests in a welcoming parade and didn't know it. When we saw what looked to be a restaurant, we hitched the horses out front of it. There was a sign above the door that said "Mr. Don's Food Place" slapped on in a hurry with red paint. We went inside.

It smelled of cabbage and onions, and I felt my appetite leave before even grabbing a chair. Franklin seemed to enjoy the reek, as he took a powerful whiff like he planned on storing the smell deep down and taking it with him. Nadine seemed indifferent.

There's no denying it was the dirtiest place I'd ever stepped foot in. The floor was covered in a scuffle-print layer of dirt, and until I finally saw a gap between the planks, I thought there was no floor at all but flattened earth from years of traffic. The walls had their own layer of dust on them, like sheer drapes, the only break in the filth being where a picture once hung.

The counter was the only thing clean. It shined like glass, as a woman polished it with a cloth in hypnotizing circles. I suppose the chore of keeping up appearances was a lot to ask for people of their age. Every living minute mattered, as did every muscle, joint, and bone.

The woman was a tiny thing with a curved spine, her smile as wide and toothless as most everyone else we'd seen so far, and she smelled of the same cabbagy-onion as her establishment. Before handing us the menu, she asked if we was only passing through. We assured her we had no intention of staying the night.

The food listed on the menu had as much appeal as everything else in the place. There was no meat. Not much of anything with substance. And after studying the list of what they offered, I realized everything was mush-like and easy to chew, like oatmeal and bread and mac and cheese—food meant for those without teeth.

I ordered the mac and cheese, while Franklin asked for bubble and squeak. Nadine ordered oatmeal with honey. The food had already been prepared, so it only took the length of time for the woman to shuffle back and forth to our table three times before we were ready to eat. I'd asked her twice if she needed a hand, but she refused the help each time. "I ain't dead yet," she'd said.

For me, the food was some of the worst I'd ever paid

for. But it filled my belly and allowed us to save what little we had left in the saddlebags. I watched Franklin feed his face and saw gratitude in him I didn't have. I figured that came from so many meals in his past being nothing more than table scraps and a whole lot of shit that wasn't fit for human consumption. Either Nadine had that same bit of gratitude, or she really did like the oatmeal, because she took every bite with no complaints, then asked for one more bowl.

CHAPTER 19

WE DECIDED IT'D be best if we hit the general store before leaving town, so we headed back, giving another nod toward the sheriff who was busy helping an old man down two rickety steps.

The store was just as dirty as the restaurant but lacked the cabbage-onion smell. It held the strong scent of perfume, like alcohol and roses. The woman who worked there was pretty for her age. I could just make out the curve in her hips before they dropped down behind the counter. Her breasts were pushed together, and between them looked like a strip of jerky. With all her teeth in order, she gave the obligatory inviting smile we were growing accustomed to in Sleepybrook.

But when she saw Franklin, she gave him a whole different kind of smile, like she meant to bed him right then and there. Her eyelids went heavy, and the corners of her mouth turned up with devilish intent. Then she ran a finger across the breast jerky and winked. Franklin saw it, cleared his throat, and looked away. He'd become quite the ladies' man on our venture. If some of the asshole men we met along the way didn't see what a treasure he was, the women sure did. Even if one of them was old enough to be his grandmother.

"Can I help you gentlemen with anything this fine afternoon?" Her voice was raspy but gentle and full of youth.

"Just thinkin' about getting some provisions, ma'am.

Thank you," Franklin said. He still didn't dare look at her and kept his eyes on the dusty shelves.

"Well, if you need anything just holler. Name's Holly."

"Actually, Holly," I said. "Now that you mention it, if you happen to sell any paper . . . " But her attention was stuck on Franklin, looking him up and down. I let her get an eyeful and asked Nadine if she'd like some candy. She said she did. I pointed out the jars of candy in varying colors on the wall opposite.

I grabbed a package of crackers, some beans, and cheese. Franklin wandered over to some hats that hung on a wooden rack. He tried one on and turned to ask Holly what the price was. His eyes went wide, and his jaw went slack. I followed his gaze and saw Holly had her tits out, long and wrinkled. She was rubbing them together like they was flint and steel, and her hips were grinding the air like maybe there was a ghostly erection there we couldn't see. If there was any question on whether or not she wanted to bed Franklin, there weren't no more.

I ran to Nadine with the hopes of blocking the bizarre sight, and she had her eyes fixed on the candy. "Pick a color," I said.

I looked over my shoulder at Franklin. He was fumbling with the hat, doing his best to ignore the woman. Then the bell above the door chimed and in walked Sheriff Shelton.

"Holly . . . tuck them things back in."

"Aww shit, Garner. You need to mind your business."

"Way I see it, this is my business. These fine folks come here to visit and what looks like pay for some goods . . . but not those goods. Now put 'em away."

Nadine swung her head around. If there's anything in this world that girl shouldn't see, she'd find a way to it.

"Nadine, pick a color," I said again. She turned toward the jars and pointed at the one filled with red candy.

Holly pushed her swinging breasts in one by one and gave another wink to Franklin, who'd put the hat back and was staring at the ground, a package of crackers in his hand.

Finally, we paid for our goods, and the sheriff walked us out. We filled our saddlebags and climbed on the horses.

"Once I saw you head in there," the sheriff said. "I knew I had to make an entrance. Holly loves her a strong negro."

"Maybe a little too much," Franklin said, and that got the sheriff to laughing until he coughed up a wad of phlegm and shot it in the dirt.

"Appreciate the hospitality, Sheriff," I said. "I think we'll be heading out now."

"You be careful through that marsh. And stay on them horses. Those gators ain't shy."

"Will do."

He patted Vengeance on the ass and walked away, tipping his hat and smiling. As we rode through town and toward the marsh, I told Franklin I was sorry about the paper.

"Ain't none of these memories I'm soon to forget. Plenty of time to write 'em down. But you know what? I wouldn't mind settling down here when I'm of age. They got a way of making you feel at home . . . long as you is wrinkled enough." Franklin gave a boisterous laugh, and it was the most pleasant thing I'd heard in days. A well-needed break from the weight that crushed us.

As we hit the edge of town, we collected the last few smiles, and I wondered if the road ahead had any more of them. Or was Sleepybrook its own bubble full of hopefuls, ignorant to the dark world just beyond its borders? One thing I knew for sure, I was glad the madman had spared the place.

CHAPTER 20

WHEN WE HIT the marsh, it was like passing through an invisible doorway. The air went thick, like molten taffy in your lungs, my skin sticky as a frog's tongue. Despite shade from the trees, the sun felt closer to the earth, as though it tired of holding itself up anymore. We stopped long enough for me to pour some water from a canteen into my handkerchief and tie it around Nadine's head. Even though she hadn't complained, I knew she was burning up in that dress.

We saw a few alligators, but they paid us no mind. I imagine with a beast like Vengeance they was intimated. Had we been on foot there'd have been a different story to tell.

The insects were loud, like they were warning the world we was coming. On a nice summer evening I might find the beauty in their song, but in the middle of that swamp, heading to a lady what some called a witch, it was nothing but a nuisance among the chaos, and I wanted to fire my gun just to see if they'd shut the hell up.

The marsh grew darker, yet the sun was far from setting, and we caught our first sign we might be on Lady Bethlehem's land—an old tree trunk with faces carved into it. A real piece of art, even if it did send spiders up my spine. The faces held no tell as to whether they was to be depicting good or evil. Just deep grooves and still eyes and mouths that both smiled and frowned. Then we saw another. And another. Then we saw stones with symbols on them, and they became more frequent until that's all we saw anymore. Symbols and faces. Finally, behind it all was Lady Bethlehem's cottage painted green with moss, like the whole place was alive and the insides were its belly.

Chickens roamed freely around the outside of the house, then somewhere in the distance I heard a hellacious squawk cut through the insects, and I just knew it was one of them birds caught in the steel jaws of a gator. The sound faded, and a woman stepped onto the broken-down porch with a shotgun in her hands.

She raised it straight at me. "You've got less than a minute to state your business."

I could see the green in the woman's eyes from where I sat, just as clear as I could the intent in them. She meant to kill.

I raised my hands slowly. "We're looking for Lady Bethlehem. If that's you, we was hoping you could help us find the man who killed my sister and hurt my niece."

She lowered the gun a little, looked at Nadine. "Who sent you?"

"The Johnston brothers."

She chuckled, then put the gun at her side, the barrel facing the porch's weathered steps. "I suspect you mean Alexander. I know that crazy brother of his sure wouldn't."

"Yes, ma'am. It was Alexander."

"Not the man-wolf," Nadine called out. This made the woman smile.

"What's your name, dear?"

"Nadine Walkinshaw."

"Come here, Nadine."

"Now hold on one second," I said, while Nadine already started off her horse. "You can't expect me to let her walk up them steps and not have my own gun at the ready."

The woman brushed a wave of red hair from her face and tucked it behind her ear. "Go ahead. I ain't fixin' to hurt her."

I grabbed my gun, slow-like, and held it at my side. I

could hear Franklin do the same. The woman leaned hers against the porch railing.

Nadine walked to the house and up the steps.

"Just look at those eyes," the woman said. She seemed to be transfixed. "You've seen a whole lot with those, haven't you, darlin'?"

Nadine nodded, then attacked the woman with a hug, and I could see her little body shake in a crying fit. The woman waved us over, then took Nadine by the hand and led her inside. We followed.

The only difference between the inside of the house and the outside was there weren't any chickens or gators inside. There was all manner of plants, some living, some dead. The dead ones hung from the ceiling by twine. In the corners of the front room were more totems with faces and symbols carved into them, and the walls were nothing but shelves, where various-sized jars dwelled. Some of the jars had what looked like herbs, some liquids, maybe medicines. A few contained things I wasn't sure I wanted to be privy to their contents. It was easy to see why people labeled this woman a witch, cuz it sure as hell looked like a home a witch might inhabit.

"Please, have a seat." Lady Bethlehem pointed toward a table surrounded by chairs. The table held four candles, a leather pouch, and a few leather-bound books. The three of us sat.

"Nadine . . . tell me what happened. Tell me everything."

"No reason to drag her through it again, ma'am. I can tell you everything you—"

"This child here is special. I need to hear it from her."

Nadine took a deep breath, then put her hands on the table and picked at the hardened drips of wax on one of the candles. "A man snuck in the house while me and my momma was sleepin'. I woke up and saw him standing over me. He was . . . he was naked."

I grabbed Nadine's hand and held it. "Nadine . . . you don't have to—"

Lady Bethlehem waved a hand at me and kept her focus on Nadine. "Go ahead, honey. I know it's difficult."

"They have their ways, Garrett," Franklin whispered. "They's strange ways, but they have 'em. Just watch." I looked at him. He seemed to be anxiously awaiting Lady Bethlehem's every word, as though any minute she'd recite some mystical words and we'd have our man served straight to us, and he didn't wanna miss it.

"He was naked, and he grabbed me. And I screamed. That's when Momma came runnin' in. She jumped on him, and they wrestled around and ended up in the other room. And Momma was cussin' that man out . . . And then she wasn't. Everything stopped. That's when the man came back in my room and . . . he had his way with me."

"That sonofabitch," Franklin grumbled.

Lady Bethlehem took Nadine's free hand in both of hers and squeezed.

"But I hurt him. When he was cuttin' Momma all up like he did, I got him right here." She pulled her hand from mine, reached over her shoulder, and touched her back. "And then he ran. Uncle Garrett showed up in the morning, and we been chasin' him ever since. He killed other people too, and now we can't find him."

"And you think I can tell you where he's at." Lady Bethlehem said.

"Yes ma'am."

"And you're fixin' to kill him, aren't you?"

Nadine sat up straight, and with conviction in her voice said, "Yes, we are."

Lady Bethlehem reached over and brushed Nadine's sweaty hair from her brown. "I'd love to help you, Nadine . . . .but in order to do that, I need something from you you're probably not gonna be able to give me."

"We'll give you anything you need, Miss Bethlehem," Franklin said.

"Do you happen to have the knife Nadine stabbed him with?"

I looked at Nadine, and she shook her head no. "What do you need that for?" I asked.

"I need a part of that man, like his hair or blood."

I rolled my eyes and stood up. "Yer as crazy as that Gabriel fella."

Franklin grabbed my wrist. "No . . . it's true, Garrett. She needs something to guide her. That's how it's done."

I knew Franklin never practiced voodoo, witchcraft, or any other hoodoo nonsense, but I knew he'd been around it, just didn't mention it much until the past few days. I had to take his word for it. I'd rather feel a fool and say I tried than walk away knowing the killer was still out there and we hadn't done a damn thing.

Lady Bethlehem's eyes fell on each of us, waiting for one of us to pull the man's blood out of our pocket like we'd been carrying it for a special occasion. Finally, Nadine did something very close to just that. She stood up, stuck her hands under her dress, and pulled her undergarments off, then set them on the table and pushed them toward Lady Bethlehem. The room was quiet as a tomb as Nadine sat back down.

Lady Bethlehem's eyes bubbled with tears, and I knew Franklin's did too, as I could hear his breath through flared nostrils while he held back. But I had a different reaction. I gritted my teeth until one of them cracked.

"Whatever it is you gotta do, you find this sonofawhore," I said. "And don't stop until you can point us in the right direction."

She nodded, then rose from her chair and went about the room collecting various jars, a book, and some of the dead herbs what hung from the ceiling. She tied the herbs together with twine, dipped them into one of the jars until they were wet, then wrapped them up in Nadine's underpants, all the while mumbling quietly to herself.

"Nadine . . . come over here with me, please." The woman reached her hand out to Nadine, and they went into the next room and sat in the middle of the floor near a large metal bowl. She put the underpants in the bowl, lit a match, and placed it on top. "Hold my hands. I want you to close your eyes and picture the man who did this to you. Everything you can remember about him. His face, his clothes. The way he smelled . . . everything. I want you to focus on all of it and nothing else."

While Lady Bethlehem mumbled more words I wasn't even sure were English, Franklin and I watched from the other room. The air filled with smoke from the smoldering bundle. I'd never smelled anything like it before. It was both pleasant and offensive, and the more of it I breathed the brighter the room got, until everything seemed to have its own personal source of light, each object detailed beyond description. Then the objects left, and I saw things that weren't there at all. Visions of bodies we'd seen along the way, my sister with her guts splayed out across the floor. Mary with hers. The corpses of flaming animals and the bullet-ridden lawmen. Even the black man who hung from the tree with his bulbous eyes gazing at nothing. Every horrible thing we'd witnessed in the past few days was laid out in front of me like some painting come to life that rotated, each image reminding me the other existed, until screams woke me from the trance.

Every one of us was screaming in terror, voices cracking under the weight of unspeakable horror. When I came to my senses, I could feel my bowels loosen like I might shit myself. I clenched, then stood and ran from the house, from the smoke, and stood on the porch, taking in the swamp air, gulping at it like water in the desert.

Behind me, the screams continued, and I could hear a deep retching from Franklin and the splash of vomit as it hit the hardwood floor. Once I caught my breath, I held it and ran back in for Nadine. Her eyes were wide, and her mouth was filled with the echoes of every perished soul she'd seen.

Lady Bethlehem's mouth held the same nightmares, but her eyes were shut tight as though straining. Tears leaked, and her brow shined with sweat.

Franklin was on his hands and knees, a line of drool connecting his mouth to the pile of vomit under him. Another flood escaped his mouth, and the pile grew.

My eyes burned from the smoke, but I froze, unable to move toward Nadine. In the moment, I tried convincing myself there was an unseen force holding me back, but it was my own fear what stopped me.

Finally, every scream stopped as though it came from a single source, and the only sound was Franklin as he coughed and spat.

I grabbed Nadine and dragged her outside by the arm—a ragdoll in my hand. She coughed, and we both drew in deep breaths of thick air. A moment later, Franklin and Lady Bethlehem joined us, both gasping, while Nadine clung to my leg and cried like a baby.

"What in the fuck was that horseshit?" I said.

Lady Bethlehem smoothed her dress out and caught her breath. "Something I hate performing more than you hate being a part of is what that was."

"I thought you was the one who was supposed to have the premonition, cuz I sure as shit did," I said.

"That's probably why my vision was so clear. I gathered all your energy, all your senses. Not just Nadine's."

"Coulda used a warning."

"If I had, would you have done it?"

I thought on it, and the answer was no.

"I feel like . . . like I drank two bottles the night before and had the kinda nightmares what could break a man," Franklin said. "The kind that make you wanna stop livin' cuz all hope is gone." His voice was shaky, and his chin quivered.

I caressed Nadine's back and asked if she was okay now. She nodded, then wiped her face but kept her arms around my leg.

"Tell me you got something out of that hell you just put us through," I said.

She fought through a smile and said, "More than I ever thought possible."

CHAPTER 21

"OKAY, LET'S HEAR IT," I waited for a line of bullshit.

"This man . . . he has a scar on his lip, doesn't he?" Lady Bethlehem said.

We hadn't told her that bit, and I could almost hear Franklin's jaw drop open like his tongue had turned to lead. Only reason mine didn't is 'cause I can be a stubborn cuss. But inside, my belly filled with crawly things that danced in fire.

"The scar splits through his mustache, and his hair is brown," she continued.

"Yes! That's him!" Nadine let go of my leg and stood up. "Where is he?"

"In my vision, I saw the elderly. Kind folks with hopeful faces. One of them is black. He's not a slave. He's a happy man. A gentle man."

"Aww shit . . . you're talking 'bout Sleepybrook. The killer's been behind us, not ahead," Franklin said.

"The man you're looking for is in a gray house, in one of the rooms. Maybe an inn."

"They don't have an inn," I said.

"Then it's a tall house, on the second floor. Don't necessarily mean he's still up there, though."

Franklin and I ran to the horses and mounted up. Nadine hugged the woman and thanked her, then mounted up too.

"God bless you, Lady Bethlehem," Franklin said.

I nodded at her, then flew like the wind through the swamp, looking back only to make sure I wasn't alone.

CHAPTER 22

BY THE TIME we got to Sleepybrook, the sun was offering its last glimpse. The streets were empty, but nearly every house on the main road had a light burning inside. When I saw the bare streets, I remembered the sheriff's bizarre threat about being there come nightfall. He'd have to deal with the intrusion this once, like it or not.

The first place I planned to visit was the sheriff's station, see if he was around. It'd save a whole lot of time having him point us toward the gray houses rather than searching in the dark.

We stopped outside his station, and I ran in while Franklin and Nadine kept their eyes on the road. There was no light inside, but the door was unlocked so I headed in, guided by the last sliver of sun. Even with that sliver, the place was dark, giving just enough light to cause a wet shine on something near the back, something on the counter where I imagined people leaned during lazy days and talked small-town gossip and told war stories of days long passed.

Half a dozen steps into the building, I knew exactly what that wet shine was. The gray, wool cat that once slept atop Sheriff Shelton's head was gone, and in its place was a smooth, bone-white dome smeared in blood that looked more black than crimson in the dull light.

I drew my gun and eyed the corners of the room, then crept around the counter. There was nothing there except the sheriff. His clothes were intact, and other than his scalp, his skin was too. I wondered if I'd interrupted the man doing his thing. So, I snuck through a back door and checked the area behind the station. I saw nothing but heard a sound I couldn't identify, then heard scuffling for sure. I froze and listened, realized the noise came from the front, where I'd left Franklin and Nadine. So, I hauled ass back through the sheriff's station. Before I even stepped foot outside, I saw Franklin on his back, his hand on his head. I stepped outside and Nadine wasn't there.

"Fuckitall, Garrett. He snuck up behind me." Franklin was trying to sit up, rubbing his head, checking for blood. There was a lot of it.

I scanned the street right and left. Didn't see so much as a moving shadow. Franklin stood up, grabbed his gun, then fell to his knees and sprayed vomit in the dirt.

"How the fuck did he get away so—"

Then I heard a door shut down the road. I swung my head and saw a two-story house. Wasn't gray. It was white, but with the moon swapping places with the sun, it'd be gray before long.

"He's in that house," I said to Franklin, then helped him to his feet and patted him on the back. I knew he'd blame himself for what happened, but I wanted him to know I didn't. "Let's go."

We got about thirty feet before gunfire shattered glass and a bullet hit the stock on Franklin's rifle, splintering it and throwing the gun from his hands. We ran for the general store behind us, and another shot was fired. Pain exploded in my foot, and I dove for the open doorway. We managed to get inside before another shot took out a window, then we crammed into the corner away from the storefront.

"You hit?" I asked through gritting teeth.

"Nope . . . but I am unarmed. Spare that pistol?"

I pulled the pistol from my side and handed it over. I still had the rifle.

Franklin saw my foot before I did. "Damn . . . you caught one."

I looked down. There was a hole at the end of my boot where blood was soaking leather. "Coulda been worse."

"Don't suppose you've got a plan?" Franklin said, getting his hand comfortable with the gun.

"Nothing besides gettin' up there as fast as our feet allow before something happens to Nadine. Not sure shooting from here is a good idea. That's a dark window up there. Could hit her instead."

Franklin peeked out the window, surveying the area, then started taking his boots off. "It's dark down here too. All these buildings casting shadows along the street. I could make my way across without him seein', slip in the house and take him out. Just gotta be quick and quiet."

"You been paying attention? You nearly got killed out there. He ain't no sloppy shot, Franklin. He sees you again, you're a dead man."

"We can't just sit here, Garrett."

"Well, if that's the only plan we got, I should be the one to go."

"Shit. You might not be as white as Nadine, but you walk out there you may as well be holdin' a torch." He nodded toward the bloody hole. "Not to mention the crippled foot."

I tried hard as I could to come up with another plan, but time wouldn't allow. Something needed doing.

"Ain't no more talkin' about it, friend. I'm headin' out." He took his shirt off and tossed it, then something caught his eye, and the horror I saw in his face had me searching the dark behind us. A moment later my face matched his. That murdering piece of shit had flayed Holly, except he didn't just take her nipples. He took the whole breast. Both of them. She was laid out, dress ripped apart, and entrails on the floor like serpents reaching out for us.

While I was caught in my shock-filled daze, Franklin ran out into the dark wearing nothing but the revolver and his pants. I readied my rifle, trying to get a look at the man in the window, but the sun had died, and moon shadows fell across the two-story house like a blanket of protection for the man inside. I searched for Franklin and could barely make him out as he crept from one shadow to the next, then disappeared altogether.

I knew within the next few minutes, someone was going to die. Life would be different. There'd be relief. Or there'd be grief. I played every scenario through my head, but the one I chose to dwell on was the one where Franklin made it upstairs and put a bullet in the man's head before he could even consider harming Nadine. I felt like a coward hiding there in the dark next to a dead woman. But if I ran into the street now and wound up dead, he'd kill Nadine for sure. Or worse.

Instead of watching and waiting, I aimed just above the window and fired, letting the pecker know we was something to fear too. The bullet hit wood, and I thought I saw a figure move inside.

"You'd better make the next one count, boy!" The man yelled from the window.

Since now we was talkin' I tried some negotiating. "The girl's been through enough. How about you let her go?"

"Already did that once. Not making the same mistake again."

I thought I caught another glimpse of Franklin crouched by a barrel. Just in front of him was a bright patch of moonlight. I prayed I wouldn't see a half-naked black man run right through it. But I did.

Light exploded in the second-story window and Franklin hit the ground, rolling out of the moonlight. The way he went down I could tell he'd been shot.

I fired another round near the window, but this time aimed for the top pane, where I knew Nadine was too short to reach should she be planted as bait. Glass shattered. Then I saw a flicker of light as the front door of the house opened and an ink-black figure slipped inside. Even wounded, Franklin had made it.

A shot rang out, and I ducked. Glass rained like

sharpened stars, covering me and the hardwood floor. I raised up and took a high wild shot to keep the distraction going while I figured Franklin searched for the stairs and the room.

"How about a trade of some sort?" My voice cracked, full of fear and desperation.

The quiet was tortuous, as I knew the next shot meant the end of someone.

I sat on my ass, the wall to my back, and looked at Holly. The lust-filled elderly woman. It seemed she had a reputation for maybe not being right in the head. But I wondered if she just had youthful passion in her that had died in the others years ago, and the only man who could feed it was a middle-aged stranger passing through town, preferably a black stranger.

Three shots broke the silence with no time between them. It was the revolver. I stood up, and pain shot through me. I ignored it and ran out the door and down the street toward the house, praying for the scenario I'd put my hope in. Or waiting for a bullet to sink my forehead.

I went through the door, stumbled in the dark toward the stairs, and followed Nadine's cry. I ran in with a finger on the trigger and saw a man face down on the floor, the back of his head wet and shiny, and Franklin against the wall, where Nadine sat with her arms around him, her face buried in his chest. Her skin seemed to glow in the moon, her eyes two lights filled with glimmering pools.

"Where'd he get you?" I knelt down in front of Franklin.

"Not in the head." He took a breath, then grunted through his next few words. "That's what really matters, don't it?"

I looked down and saw he was holding his stomach. His fingers glistened.

"Dammit, Franklin . . . " I sat beside him, gave my back to the wall, and we both stared ahead at the body on the floor.

"Was the only way, Garrett." He coughed, and I felt the spray of blood hit me. "And look at us now. We did it."

"You did it, my friend."

He coughed, and more blood sprayed. "Hell, if it weren't for you and Nadine I'd be hanging from a tree. We did this . . . together."

We let the silence speak for a moment, then he said, "Funny thing is . . . I really like this little town. Figured I'd plant my feet here once I got enough gray on my head. Figured I'd . . . " His breathing was rapid, his words hard to hear. "Figured I'd die here one day . . . And yet here I am."

"You ain't getting out that easy. This is one hell of a story you have to write yet." And even though I'd heard his final breath leak out like a whisper to God that he was ready now, I kept on talkin'. I talked about how we was gonna add onto that shithole shack of his and the steaks we'd eat and the drink we'd down and how it was only a matter of time before he found himself a wife because the ladies sure did take to him. But when the words began to feel like nothin' but a breath of dust being carried by the wind, I screamed until my throat was raw and tasted like bile. And that's when every tear I'd been holding, since I saw my sister dead, came out in a flood.

Nadine held me, and I held her, and we cried together.

Until a moan that came from neither of us filled the dark room.

As though she were already waiting, Nadine grabbed Franklin's gun and started shooting at the man on the floor. Every bullet went through skull, and she pulled the trigger over and over until the only sound left was the empty click of the hammer.

Next thing we heard was the sound of shuffling feet and chatter in the streets, then the creak of steps under old feet as the kind folks from Sleepybrook headed up the stairs.

CHAPTER 23

WE BURIED FRANKLIN that next morning right there in Sleepybrook. It was the one place that treated him fairly. Anywhere else, and it seemed you're bound to find a least a few assholes who think a man ain't a man unless he looks like them.

I helped the townsfolk carry the man with the cleft lip out of the bedroom, then we pushed him down the stairs. As we did so, I took note of the strange necklace he wore. The whole thing was made from nipples. My sister's were in there somewhere.

He also wore a vest and chaps that at first glance looked like a drunk had taken up sewing, as the stitching was crude, and every swatch was a different shade. But when I saw parting lips that held a button, I knew for sure it was human flesh.

Folks scavenged his saddlebags and found them stuffed with human skin, some of which was tanned and treated, some still wet with gore. Sheriff Shelton's scalp was stuck in there too. It'd been filled with apples like some kind of pouch.

They unhitched the horse and slapped its ass—which was covered in a long strip of flesh—sending the thing on its way, calling it a bad omen that no one should ever ride again.

When the horse was gone, we dragged the killer into the street and lit the fucker on fire. After he burned to the bone, a few of the older men whipped their shriveled cocks out and pissed on his smoldering body.

We ate with the townsfolk and listened to their memories of Holly and the Sheriff, and I shared a few about Franklin.

On the way home, Nadine and I stopped at Franklin's shithole shack and grabbed his books and every story I could find. The next few days I spent organizing the stories and putting them in order to form a collection. The man had a real talent. Spelling was bad as ever, but he was one hell of a writer.

Within the next two years, I was able to find a publisher to release the collection in a small paperback. While the book was in Franklin's name, they didn't allow for a proper biography for fear of it not selling on account of his color. So, I did the best I could and wrote an introduction in my name, talking about the man I knew.

The best man I ever knew.

ACKNOWEDGEMENTS

Other than thanking my wife for her masterful cheerleading prowess, I'd like to thank Jarod Barbee and Patrick Harrison III at Death's Head Press for listening to my pitch and believing in me enough to send a contract without having seen a word of this book, as a word hadn't been written. Jeremy Wagner and Steve Wands for their patience and aid in making sure this sees the light of day. Justin Coons for the gorgeous cover. The rest of my gratitude goes to my patrons (listed below), and to the two authors I drew inspiration from while writing this book: Joe R. Lansdale and John Boden. Patrons: (Your support is encouraging, inspiring, and priceless) Michael Perez, Shannon Bradner, George "Book Monster" Ranson, Liane Abe, Steve Gracin, Wayne Fenlon, Vitina Molgaard, Connie Bracke, Mathieu Fortin, John Questore, Danielle Milton, Beth Lee, Mary Kiefel, Dirk Gard, Tim (CaptainTrips), Lee-ann Oleski, Levi Walls, Stewie (Steve Pattee), Glenda Magner, Jamie Goecker, Jerri Nall, Night Worms (Sadie and Ashley), Melissa Potter, Shannan Ross, Richard Martin, Kristyn Kasper, Alyssa Manning, Sheila Porter, Holly Rae Garcia, Phillip Frangules, Crystal Lake Publishing (Joe Mynhardt), Justin G., Crystal Staley, Hunter Shea, Cyndie Randall, Jon Cowles, Missy Kritzer, Tina True Edwards, Alexis Vieira, and Justas Grigas.

ABOUT THE AUTHOR

Covering crime, thrillers, dark drama, horror, and even the humorous, Chad's short fiction can be found in several dozen magazines and anthologies, and some of his books include: *Of Foster Homes & Flies, Stirring the Sheets, Cannibal Creator, Skullface Boy, The Pale White*, and *The Neon Owl* series. Lutzke's work has been praised by authors Jack Ketchum, Richard Chizmar, Joe R. Lansdale, Stephen Graham Jones, Tim Waggoner, and his own mother. He can be found lurking the internet at www.chadlutzke.com